I0575309

Anonymous

Episodes in the Life of an Indian Chaplain

Anonymous

Episodes in the Life of an Indian Chaplain

ISBN/EAN: 9783337071073

Printed in Europe, USA, Canada, Australia, Japan

Cover: Foto ©Raphael Reischuk / pixelio.de

More available books at **www.hansebooks.com**

EPISODES IN THE LIFE OF AN INDIAN CHAPLAIN.

BY

A RETIRED CHAPLAIN.

KAMPTEE CEMETERY ENTRANCE.

London:

SAMPSON LOW, MARSTON, SEARLE, & RIVINGTON,

CROWN BUILDINGS, 188, FLEET STREET.

1882.

[All rights reserved.]

Dedicated ·

TO THE MEMORY OF

MOTHER AND CHILDREN,

WHO REST IN JESUS IN THE

FAR-OFF LAND.

INTRODUCTION.

SOME few words of apology seem to be necessary for submitting to the Public the personal work of an Indian Chaplain, and who for that very reason desires to be unnamed.

In the first sixteen years of the author's residence abroad, he was encouraged, sustained, and helped by one, who has now entered into her rest.

The duties of Indian Chaplains are of a peculiar kind; sent out to minister to the spiritual wants of the European troops, much other work presents itself for acceptance.

Missionary work, in a modified form, is always at hand, and exertions on behalf of the Eurasian community more than ever urgent, since the educational efforts of the Government have been solely with a view to benefit the *native* population. If his example, in its small degree, in a missionary and educational point of view, should stir up his brother chaplains to extend their duties as far as practicable in these directions, the author will be amply recompensed for his labours in recalling many a sad and sorrowful, as well as amusing and instructive incident in a busy life.

The design figured on the cover of the book represents an elephant, surmounted by two fanciful monsters; the highest and largest of which resembles a horse with the trunk of an elephant. It is called by the Hindoo poets an *aullee*, and is a favourite subject for representation in carving throughout Travancore.

With regard to the illustrations, the author's thanks are especially due to the wife of General Gordon, for her spirited sketch of the Marble Rocks at Jubbulpore, taken midst many difficulties on the spot.

To Mrs. Gilbert-Cooper, for her truthful sketch of a " Shola " on the Neilgherry Hills, his thanks are also due.

Through the kindness of Colonel Marshall, the author has been able to place before the reader three sketches of "Todas," already published in his interesting and valuable book called "A Phrenologist amongst the Todas."

His thanks are also due to two of his dear children for many drawings which now appear. And lastly, he is indebted to the courtesy of his publishers for several illustrations which they have kindly placed at his disposal.

Commenced in loneliness, in a strange land, far away from his children, these pages were sketched for their edification and put aside, and only in the hope of furthering their education and welfare resumed, and now placed before the public in the hope that they may be found acceptable.

CONTENTS.

CHAPTER I.

CHAPTER II.

CHAPTER IX.

CHAPTER X.

CHAPTER XI.

Contents.

LIST OF ILLUSTRATIONS.

xvi   *List of Illustrations.*

EPISODES

LIFE OF AN INDIAN CHAPLAIN.

CHAPTER I.

School incident—Home life—University—Diaconate—
First curacy—Curious relic of a bygone age—
Priesthood and change of curacy—Pets—Peculiar
habit of a dog—"A larger scene of action is displayed"—Surplicing a country choir—Missionary
college and discipline—Long vacation—Affecting
incident—Windsor—Chatham and its hostelry—Low
life and rescue—Mary the penitent—Appointment
to East Indian chaplaincy—Marriage—departure
for the East.

"Do thy part with thy *industry*, and let God point
the *event*.

"I have seen *matters* fall out so *unexpectedly*, that
they have tutored me in all *affairs*, neither to *despair*,
nor *presume:* Not to *despair; for God can help* me:
Not to *presume; for God can cross* me."

FELLTHAM'S RESOLVES.

B

BORN half a century ago, my first recollections of life bring me to my mother's knees, the confidante of all my childish joys and sorrows.

The youngest son of a professional man of eminence, I had little, with several sisters, to expect, beyond a decent education and my father's blessing. All this I in due course received; how and in what manner will be briefly shown.

I was entered at a public school, and one irresistibly comic scene still presents itself to my memory, with which I shall favour the reader. A young scholar, a mere child into whom learning had been prematurely crammed, was at fault in his lesson. He was a little bit of a fellow, with a most sensitively nervous temperament.

Imagine then the master, a perfect Goliath in stature, standing over the delinquent boy, and demanding why the lesson had not been properly prepared. The poor child at last, in agony, cried out, "Beat me! Oh, kick me! Nurse (*the good woman*) hid my book away." I knew not, boy as I was, whether to laugh or to cry.

My home life was a very happy one, blessed beyond measure in my parents and brothers and sisters; living in the very heart of London, in a bright and cheerful spot, although yclept " the valley of the shadow of death " from the number of doctors there resident, with the beautiful parks of Hyde and St. James', near at hand, my early years passed rapidly away. It was no small pleasure to get a scamper over Primrose Hill or Hampstead Heath, with the flappers and insect collecting-box, bringing home stores to amuse leisure hours.

All my leisure time was given to my different collections of natural history and antiquities, little anticipating how useful all such knowledge would prove to me in after-years. It is unnecessary to dwell upon my college days, where with the toga I assumed the " light blue tie." It was a joyous time, not a care, or a sigh, or a tear. Yes; one care, the desire to attain the wishes of my early years, and try and do " The Divine Master's " work.

My father gave me my choice of a profession, and so I entered into Holy Orders. The influences of a university life were all, on a mind bent upon such a profession, for good. Perhaps the wine parties in those days were a little too frequent, but the pleasure of intercourse with kindred spirits, all in the hey-day of life and joyous anticipation, was thoroughly enjoyable.

The constitutional, or ride, boating or cricket, after lectures, and the necessary study for the periodic examinations made the three years glide away, and found me studying for the Diaconate.

That ordeal was passed soon after leaving college; one more trial, and then no more forced burning of the "midnight oil," but a steady diligence in the studies wherein my soul delighted.

Those were days when men entered into holy orders as a profession, and it was no difficult matter to obtain a pass. There was only one, or at the most two, theological colleges in existence, and they were considered by many as valuable aids to candidates for the ministry.

At that time they were considered by some to have a narrowing effect upon the mind, and were for the most part only resorted to by men who had not thought much of their future profession.

Though I did not enter one, it has always been to me a matter of regret; for I am persuaded that it would have the effect of deepening the spiritual life, and if perchance any unreality was engendered, the reality would come soon enough.

It does come, when one finds one's self fighting against the powers of darkness, ignorance, and the neglect of souls, in a past generation.

I have preached my first sermon, read the prayers, without forgetting the psalms, bidden adieu to my father's house with all its love and care and prayers, and find myself ensconced in a rude and not very picturesque farm-house.

I have been ordained deacon with as little formality and with as little to touch the heart as was possible, in a small out-of-the-way chapel in Regent Street.

The bishop was a grand old man, beaming with kindness, but rather past his work. He had been, when a young man, from his handsome person styled the "beauty of holiness."

I was in sole charge of a small parish of about 120 people, assisted once a quarter by a neighbouring priest, and " passing rich " on 50*l.* a year. The rector, who held the living for a minor, paid a quarterly visit to the parish, when I and the School Dame received our rich emoluments.

The church was a small, unpretending edifice, with shingled spire, and with nothing of antiquarian interest about it, with the exception of one object; it had a stand for an hour-glass on the left-hand side of the pulpit and the north side of the church.

This curious relic of a past age reminds me of an amusing anecdote of a country squire who lived in the times when they were " three-bottle men," and any one who could not stow away as much under his girdle was little accounted of.

His companion was the minister who probably had suffered more than once from the
ill-judged hospitality of his friend's pressing
invitation to take—

" A flagon more,
To drench dry cares, and make the welkin roar."

After one of these orgies, he, it is related,
avenged himself on the following Sunday,
when at the conclusion of an hour's discourse, and looking at the squire, he turned
the hour-glass and grimly said, " Let us,
my brethren, take ' *one glass more,*' " probably to the infinite dismay of his late
host.

"Here, waiter, more wine ! let me sit while I'm able,
Till all my companions sink under the table."

Apart from the " hour-glass," the church
may be best described in the words of the
Rev. W. Heygate,—

"Cushions and cloth and books, takin' the old church
right roun',
Surplice, shovel and broom, they would na' fetch'd
half-a-crown,

Commandments to boot.   They was the only good
    lookin' things,
Wi' yellow cherubs between 'em, and nout but heads
    and wings ;
Parson Miles was a preacher, and could gallop through
    a prayer,
Right straight-a-head on anything, an' stop him who
    dare."

The quiet twelvemonth I rusticated here
was a good opportunity for studying for
priest's orders. Of course I over-shepherded
the people ; and if I did no particular good, I
do not think much harm came to them from
my inexperience.

Having entered the priesthood, I prepared to quit my first charge for "fresh
fields and pastures new," and the conventional 100*l.* sterling per annum.

My new rector was a fine specimen of the
Squarson type. A real old English gentleman, but now totally invalided with that aris-
tocratic enemy, the gout. With what gusto
he would narrate a burst with the "Bark-
shire hounds." He was a sound Churchman
of the old school, he never visited his people,
as he held the doctrine that every English-

man's house is his castle. Of course he
went on emergency, and many an infant was
ushered into the Church's fold in his
brougham.

The days were only then just expiring
when "pluralities" were in vogue. Many a
tale have I heard of the third service at a
third church, and in one well-authenticated
occasion of the parson leaping his horse over
the churchyard wall, and tying him up in the
belfry.

Those days have happily passed away,
and left us a body of men who, if more self-
assertive, amongst its younger members is
certainly better trained, more earnest, self-
denying, and active.

The parish I now had charge of was partly
rural and partly urban. The church was
situated in the rural part on the summit of
a hill surrounded with magnificent old yew-
trees.

Its fine, massive, ivy-covered, square
tower overlooked sloping fields of corn,
and commanded a view of the old rectory,
which nestled midst shrubs and evergreens.

The farmer in whose house I lodged kept his hunter, and always had a useful cob at the disposal of the parson.

I had some pet dogs, my companions at my lonely dinner-table. They were very small bull-terriers, of excellent tempers and such tails. "Why, sir," said a dog-fancier to me one day, "*them dogs' tails are as smooth and tapering as a tobacco-pipe.*"

The head of this family had a peculiar habit inherited from his grandfather, for he was a dog of pedigree. He allowed a favourite "pussy" just to put her nose to any choice morsel I had thrown her, when he would jump with a sudden spring upon her back, and coolly having thus frightened her away, gobble up the *morceau* himself; and so is the distich true,—

"Who ne'er so tame, so cherish'd and lock'd up,
Will have a wild trick of his ancestors."

My life for some three years was an active and pleasant one. In the urban part of my parish I had to encounter the dissenting grocer, and polemics ensued. I do not remember many conquests on my part, though I was sufficiently earnest to have my church well filled. I believe my life won more converts than my divinity.

Hitherto I had been working alone, and it is not good for man to be alone, so I accepted a curacy in another county, where I had the companionship of my rector and a fellow-curate, whose friendship I still have the pleasure of retaining.

Frequent services, weekly celebrations, a fine organ, and a good choir could not be resisted.

The church was a very fine one, consisting of nave and two side aisles, an Anglo-Norman tower, and two side chapels. When restored by the preceding rector, the Rev. Dr. Barret, a scholar and divine, mural paintings were discovered of a most interesting character.

There was also a curious alms-box of oak. It stood about three feet in height, let into a beam of oak, bound with iron bands, the intervening spaces being studded with small pebbles, to prevent the action of a chisel.

There were the usual three clasps for padlock, for rector and churchwardens.

CURIOUS ALMS-BOX.

My new rector was an excellent musician, rather eccentric at times, and the inheritor of a rich family living. He was of a very practical turn of mind. Visiting him one day, after that great event, the surplicing of a country choir, he said, " I have just received a deputation who object to the men and boys being surpliced."

" How did you manage them ? " I asked.

" I think I have settled the matter," he replied. " I said, ' Gentlemen, I have a great objection to seeing the boys in dirty jackets ; but if you will engage twice a year to clothe them decently, I will take off the surplices.' "

He heard no more of the objection, and was fortunate in not having had his curate present, who probably would have argued the matter on other grounds, and raised a case for the ecclesiastical courts to decide.

The parish was a very large one, and its out-lying hamlets made the work very trying.

After about three years' work, having a fellowship offered to me at a missionary college, I accepted it, and again removed my tent.

I was very much induced to take this step from having heard some striking discourses by the late Bishop Selwyn, when at Cambridge, which had opened my mind to life abroad.

I now look back through a long vista of years, and am thankful for the discipline which the college imparted to teacher and scholar alike. I learnt to be self-denying and punctual, to husband my time watchfully, and it brought me into contact with the truest-hearted Churchmen and the best of men.

MISSIONARY COLLEGE.

The college was, though situated in a city, in a quiet and secluded spot, a spot very dear to English Churchmen, with the Angel Tower of the cathedral looking down on its well-kept grassy quadrangle.

" It had been built on the ruins of an old abbey, and was rescued from the most degrading and profane uses by the liberality of Mr. Beresford-Hope, who purchased them and presented them to the Church of England, for purposes akin to those for which they were founded."

The work was full of deep interest. The day began and ended with chapel. There were lectures from nine to one o'clock, then printing-press, gardens, carpentry, and hospital work all to be attended to.

Every Saint's Day there was a general holiday, in which both teacher and taught found relaxation. In the Long Vacation it was customary for one of the fellows to reside, to look after foreign students. It was my turn to be thus employed. The city in its more crowded parts had been for some time unhealthy, and conservancy was not so much attended to as it happily is now.

A city incumbent, who had formerly been one of the fellows of the college, was ordered abroad, and I consented to take his duty. No sooner had he gone than cholera broke out in his district, and I had to bury several of his parishioners.

At one of these funerals I noticed a young woman in a paroxysm of grief, and sent for her to the vestry.

I then learnt that she had lost a favourite companion from the disease very suddenly. She told me that in the house where she was lodging there were fourteen of these poor girls, maintained by the publican (*and sinner*) for the gain they brought him by their presence.

The death of Mary's companion, for such I shall call her, had greatly startled her. And she was most earnestly desirous of changing her life if she could find the opportunity. She also stated that one of her companions was of the same mind. I agreed to meet her the next day at a small public-house in the city, and make the necessary arrangements. Meantime I arranged with one of the most experienced of the neighbouring clergy to accompany me on my errand.

We accordingly met at the " Pottikin " on

the following day, and Mary promised to accompany me to a penitentiary near London.

Her friend, however, would have nothing to say to this project. I shall never forget the poor girl's voice and manner. In the most tragic way she said, "No! NO! *I once knew a gal who was took to one of them penitentiaries, they fed her on rice and water,* AND SHE WAS NEVER HEARD OF AGAIN!"

Nothing we could urge moved her, and we had to be content with our one poor little bird. Our bird, however, was not quite in hand yet, though through the kindness of one of the canons of the cathedral, I had procured a nomination to a London penitentiary for my penitent.

A regiment had just returned from Burmah; prize-money had been distributed; in one public-house a corporal and three privates spent 20*l.* one night, and the city exhibited anything but a seemly aspect.

The British soldier did not appear under favourable colours, or as the disciple of Father Matthew.

It was deemed advisable to send the

regiment away, and they were, as I understood, ordered to Windsor.

In the meantime an officer's servant induced
Mary to accompany him, and she went.
When I heard this my first feeling was bitter
disappointment and sorrow on her account,
my second was the reflection that these poor
girls, from the lawlessness of their lives,
most frequently act on the impulse of the
moment.

There was no time for hesitation, and off
I started for Windsor. On arriving there I
was not a little chagrined to find the orders
had been countermanded for Chatham, and
so to Chatham I went.

I found the officers' quarters, and inter-
viewed the servant. I pleaded Mary's cause
effectually, and he gave me her direction. I
soon found myself in the slums of Chatham,
and discovered the public-house I was in
search of. I walked straight into the bar,
and, as good fortune would have it, found
the landlady at the " receipt of custom."

I asked for Mary, and said I wanted to see
her. The landlady said, " I see, sir, you are

a clergyman. I am so glad you have come, the poor girl has been in such a taking, and reproaching herself so, for coming away." On this she led me upstairs alone. I found Mary, and a second Mary; she evinced great pleasure at seeing me, and burst into tears. A few kind words set her at ease, and we then in conclave settled what was to be done.

There was fortunately a coach which would start in the course of the day, and in this we decided to go. I sent the landlady out to buy a shawl, a bonnet, and a pocket-handkerchief; and these obtained, off we started as fast as four good horses could take us.

To this day I cannot call to mind my reasons for ordering a pocket-handkerchief, which Mary was to carry in her hand. It had, I suppose, in my cerebellum something of a Sunday-like look about it, without the Prayer Book; anyhow it formed a quasi sign of respectability in my mind at that time.

Probably at the present day, had I to give similar directions, I should say, "Purchase good woman, a dress with at least three or

four colours in it, which will tie in a bundle
behind; a pair of high-heeled boots, a mass
of false hair, and a very small ·pocket-
handkerchief to be placed mayhap on the
crown of the head !

We reached our destination by eventide,
and the college porter's wife found lodgings
for the poor girl, quite as pleased as myself
at the result of my expedition.   Next day we
started for London, where I left my charge
under very good care.

I will now briefly narrate the final termi-
nation of this occurrence.   Poor Mary ! born
and bred in the country, too long· accustomed
to have her own way, pining for the green
fields and pretty hop-gardens from which she
had never been far distant, wearied with the
constraint of the London penitentiary, ran
away *to her mother*.

The poor girl was in a rapid decline; her
mother took her in and sent for my good
friend the Canon, through whose instru-
mentality she had been placed in the penitentiary.   The good Canon attended her for
some time, when she was called away from

this world, and I heard, for I was then in India, that she died most penitent, sending to me, with her latest breath, her love.

Thus died Mary the Penitent, aged *nineteen.* I have mentioned a second Mary. I went to Ramsgate to see her mother, and induce her to take her daughter back. This she utterly refused to do. We had a very stormy meeting, and I left, wiping off the dust of my feet, *figuratively,* at her door.

I returned to college and read accidentally, if I may so speak, an article in the *Quarterly* on Indian Chaplaincies. This induced me to pay Leadenhall Street a visit, and get a list of the Directors of the Honourable East India Company.

Four months after this visit, through the kind offices of my friend the Canon, I obtained a chaplaincy, having had my choice of Presidency, and elected that of Madras.

I parted with regret from the students, for the greater part of them were earnest men, ready to hazard their lives for the Gospel's sake. Too many, to outward seeming, have now passed away young in years, but ripe for the kingdom they were teaching others to attain unto.

I now commenced preparations for my departure. Having resigned my fellowship, a two years' engagement with her who was to be my partner in life for the following sixteen years, ended in a happy marriage.

In those days it was considered a serious business preparing for a voyage to India. I was advised to go by the Cape of Good Hope, as that was supposed to acclimatize the constitution better than the more rapid inland route.

We enjoyed a pleasant cathedral tour, varied by a visit to the Cumberland lakes, and ending with one to the good Warden at the college. We received the full congratulations of Warden and Fellows, the students taking good care to intimate to me that they approved of my choice.

How kind and sympathizing they all were ! We felt that the bond which had united us in a common work would not be altogether severed by my new appointment, and that some of us would meet again in the far East, (they labouring amongst the native population) with many experiences to relate, and which occurred on several occasions. And nobly I found in after-years, were they fulfilling their duties, an ample reward for their careful and painstaking training.

> " Be the day ever so long
> At last it ringeth to evensong."

And so our holiday came to an end, and we started in the good ship *Barham* for the East.

CHAPTER II.

Voyage—Madras—Landing and its incidents—Fort St.
George—St. Mary's and its monuments—Style of
houses—Reception—State of religious parties—Re-
porting arrival—Visit to the Bishop's palace—
Cathedral—Ordered to Rangoon—*En route*—Cal-
cutta, "the City of Palaces"—Garden Reach—
Bishop's College—Eastern hospitality—Johnny the
Chinaman as shoemaker—Arrival of European
troops—Amusing scene—China bazār—The shilling
razor, or Birmingham in the East—Voyage to
Rangoon — Arrival — Shops — Houses — Bazārs—
Gnapee, country "caviare."—Shwe-Dagon pagoda—
Description—Buddhism—Running coachman.

"Here are two pilgrims,
And neither of them knows one footstep of the way."
HEYWOOD.

"That a man may better himself by *Travael*, he ought
to observe and comment: noting as well the *bad* to
avoid it; as taking the *good* into use. And without
Registering these things by the *Pen*, they will slide away
unprofitably.

"A man would not think, how much the *Characterizing*

of a *thought* in *Paper* fastens it. LITERA SCRIPTA
MANET has a large sense. He that does this may, when
he pleaseth, rejourney all his *Voyage* in his *Closet.*"

FELLTHAM'S RESOLVES.

The voyage occupied rather more than four
months. We had a pleasant and skilful captain and agreeable passengers, and amongst
them we made the acquaintance of a Calcutta
merchant and his daughter, of whom I shall
have to speak anon.

We have arrived in the Madras Roads, and
I have received an official letter telling me
that I am appointed chaplain of Rangoon in
Burmah.

After so long a voyage this was not very
gratifying news, but as I accepted the appointment with the intention of going where
I was sent, it simply resolved itself into a
question of time.

I was asked to take up my quarters with
the Fort chaplain, until I had seen the
bishop and arrangements were made for my
departure for British Burmah.

When we arrived in the Roads it was too
hot to land, so that we had to wait for even-

tide. The intermediate time passed rapidly away, no small portion of our attention being taken up with noticing the Massoolah and Catamaran boatmen.

We had to bid adieu to our fellow-passengers, and witness the meeting of parents who for years had been separated from their children.

We landed, but who can describe the scene of confusion! The chaplain's butler had secured a horse-gharrie for us, a species of London four-wheeler, drawn by a horse of most rat-like proportions, but showing " blood " at all points.

Our hopes of getting away quickly, though thus provided for, were far from being speedily realized. What a crush of natives! all jabbering and sahib-ing around us. " There they talk. Ye gods, how they do talk."

No sooner was a portmanteau placed on the vehicle than some one of these dusky sons of the soil seized it piecemeal, and placed it in his own conveyance. It had to be recovered, and even this tedious process

ended at last, and we proceeded on our way
to the Fort.

The Fort did not appear to me to be a
very formidable fortress. It is a large and
handsome enclosure, with a fine block of
public buildings for Government offices.

Barracks for the troops, with upper stories,
furnished in front and rear with verandahs,
and which takes away the naked appearance of such buildings presented to us
in England.

Houses for Government officers and the
chaplain, an arsenal, and the church, completed the picture.

The latter is a fine old structure, not at all
ecclesiastical in appearance, built of laterite.
It has some interesting marble monuments,
and, amongst others, one to the memory
of the celebrated Schwartz, the Apostolic
missionary.

The lower portions of the houses seemed
to be used as godowns, or places for stowing
away goods, the upper stories alone being
available for dwelling in. The usual construction appeared to be one very long,

broad, and lofty room, divided by a centre
archway and screen, which made them ser-
viceable as drawing and dining room.   The
rooms on either side were used as bed,
dressing, and bath rooms.

The Fort was surrounded by a moat with
drawbridge.   Arrived at the house, we were
ushered into the large drawing-room.   It
had an unfurnished look about it, the floors
being covered with rattan matting, and the
walls of white polished chunam, very much
like white marble.

This composition is made out of lime
manufactured from sea shells, and plastered
a quarter of an inch in thickness on the walls,
smoothed by a trowel, and afterwards with
an agate, which gives it a beautiful polish.

There was no host to receive us, and we
had to wait for some time ere he appeared.
He had been attending a most interesting
prayer-meeting.   I am not going to enter
here upon a dissertation as to the efficacy of
united prayer ; but probably my indulgent
reader will agree with me in thinking that
" mine host " would have offered a more

acceptable sacrifice, had he been present to receive strangers in a strange land, with a welcome in person.

Had the good man—and he was really a good man—been engaged at evensong no objection could have been taken to his absence. But he was one of the leaders of a religious clique then very powerful in Madras.

We felt chilled, and congratulated ourselves on that which we had been rather deploring, our mission to British Burmah. Excepting this little slip on the part of our host, he was most hospitable and kind, and showed every attention to guests whose opinions were diametrically opposed to his own.

The first morning at breakfast we saw abundance of well-dressed servants, who moved noiselessly about, and attended thoroughly to our wants.

I ventured to ask if they were Christians. "*No*," he replied, "*some are heathen, some Roman Catholic, which is much the same.*"

A rapid glance from my dear wife warned me, and I held my peace.

The state of religious parties in those days was not very harmonious. It was a struggle rather between ultra-evangelicalism and utter carelessness or indifference. There were certain churches to which the newly arrived chaplain or missionary was bidden, or the reverse.

I found myself left to my own devices, much to my own private satisfaction.

I was now instructed to report my arrival to the authorities, and amongst others to the Town Major. I did as I was bidden, but discovered afterwards that I had been sent to the latter important functionary to be reported upon *in religious circles*. I was to visit the bishop, receive my licence for Burmah, pay ecclesiastical dues, preach in the cathedral, and wind up by dining at the episcopal table.

We are now on our way to the palace at " The Adyar," a distance of some eight miles from the Fort.

The heat and glare—for everything seemed to us of dazzling whiteness—appeared to us excessive, and this was the *cold* weather of

Madras. What would the hot weather prove?

The good bishop received us most kindly, and the cool rooms were a pleasant change from the exterior heat and dust. We, that is the Fort chaplain and myself, then retired to the bishop's sanctum, to take the canonical oaths, *et cetera.*

I was here introduced to a most oleaginous personage, the registrar of the diocese.

He was a short, stout man, of florid complexion, seemingly on the verge of an apoplectic seizure. He had a habit of casting his eyes up to the ceiling and groaning; possibly this gave him relief from some internal complaint, for he was not at all a bad kind of a fellow, enjoyed a good dinner, and forgot his groans when warmed up with the episcopal champagne.

I had taken the oaths, been assured of the salubrity of Rangoon, and the pleasantness of the charge (though, by-the-bye, it had the repute of being a second Botany Bay), when up rose the bishop, who having

"By his countenance
Enjoin'd me silence."

thus "prepared to speak,"—

"I HOPE NOW THAT YOU HAVE COME OUT TO INDIA YOU WILL PREACH THE GOSPEL."

I was rather taken aback; however I replied earnestly, "*My lord, I was sent out for that express purpose.*" Whether his lordship thought me beyond redemption, or that I had better be left alone, I know not; we had no more polemics, wherein I rejoiced.

I had already had a taste of the MADRAS GOSPEL, and it was not at all suited to my palate.

I had been residing amongst true-hearted Churchmen, loving and learned, and my soul loathed anything approaching to unreality. Because I had been one of this fraternity I was excluded from some of their churches, and the bishop was induced to relegate me to his Botany Bay.

The next day I preached at the cathedral. The mind episcopal in those days had not arrived at the due order of processionals.

After, therefore, a prayer in the vestry, I was rebuked for placing myself first, being under the impression that it was the post of humility, so the first became last, and the bishop, like many of his warlike predecessors, led the van.

The Madras cathedral, five and twenty years ago, was in a very different state to that in which it is now. A huge ungainly structure of brick and mortar, outwardly plastered, was fitted up with large and cumbrous pews; a huge reading-desk and pulpit in one, formed the presiding deities of the temple. The altar was completely obscured.

Prayers and sermon over, at which the bishop expressed his approbation, we returned to the palace for dinner.

The drive was a very enjoyable one, the fine broad roads, the huge bamboo and casuarina-trees, the quaint grass-thatched, or leaf-thatched huts, here and there, the pretty fire-flies, flitting through the heavily-scented air from the flowering trees and shrubs, were all alike novel and enchanting to us.

D

It was a pleasant drive enough, and the good bishop, a real prince at his hospitable board, was kindness itself. Such was the last interview with my diocesan.

I was not able to pronounce the Madras shibboleth, and so I was transferred for many years to come to the most distant stations in the Presidency.

We had now been five days in Madras, and there seemed no likelihood of getting a vessel direct to Rangoon.

I was anxious to see as much as possible of India, and had a particular desire to visit " *The City of Palaces*," Calcutta, so I requested permission to proceed thither by the *Barham*.

This was granted, and a free passage given me, and so we found ourselves again at sea. In spite of its ten feet square size, how acceptable was the cabin on the wide, wide sea to us, after all the excitement, the jabber, the dust, and the glare, with the *thermometer* at 80°, and the *ecclesiastical* higher still, of the Presidency town.

We had a very pleasant voyage to Calcutta,

and a pressing invitation from our merchant friend, Mr. Ilberry, and his daughter, to stay with them, until we could obtain a company's vessel to take us to Rangoon.

Our friends lived in " GARDEN REACH," on the banks of the Hoogly, and exactly opposite to " BISHOP'S COLLEGE," a strikingly English structure, designed for the instruction of native candidates for the ministry of the " CHURCH OF ENGLAND." It was a pretty sight to see these palatial residences dotted all along the banks of the river, with their beautiful gardens reaching down to the water's edge.

Our friend lived in princely style, the house was large and commodious, the hall paved with marble of different colours, and a wide-sweeping staircase leading to the drawing and bed rooms. Below was the dining-room.

The house was most elegantly furnished with all kinds of works of art and vertu, and flowers in abundance in every direction. The servants, whose number seemed legion, were dressed in their flowing white robes, with embroidered belts across their shoulders, and their master's crest in silver on their turbans.

My friend said to me, on welcoming me, from the *budgerow* or covered boat, " *Now, padre, you are to go your own way and I must go mine, we shall always meet at breakfast and dinner. There is a close carriage for you, and a palanquin and bearers. My daughter will be pleased to take you and your wife for the evening drive.*"

Charming quarters ! unaffected hospitality, and when we parted at the end of a fortnight it was with much regret.

The " City of Palaces " has been so frequently described, that it needs no description at my hands. What a marvellous mixture it was of *splendour* and *squalor !*

One quarter of an hour you are driving past " Government House," with perhaps, according to the season, a line of those queer-looking, long-legged birds called the " adjutant " perched on its abutments, or along a splendid row of mansions, many-storied ; and in another quarter of an hour you find

VILLAGE SCENE.

Page 37.

yourself in a narrow roadway, with leaf-
thatched huts on either side, the occupants
of which are retailing for a few copper coins
their stores of "betel leaf" and chunam,
grain and ghee,—

" The traders cross-legg'd midst their spice and grain,
   The housewives bearing water from the well,
   The weaver at his loom, the cotton bow
   Twanging, the mill-stones grinding meal,
   The dyers stretching waist-cloths in the sun,
   Wet from the vats,"

very far removed from the plate glass and
sashed windows of their European neighbours.

The merchant's daughter had been absent
from India about ten years, but in a week's
time was talking Hindustani with tolerable
fluency to the native servants. The natives
in Bengal all converse in this language, and
not in broken English as their Madras
brethren.

There are a great many nationalities represented in Calcutta, and amongst others a
large number of Chinamen.

We were told that they excelled in carpentry and shoemaking, that boots and shoes manufactured by them were almost equal to those sent from France. So my wife determined on ordering some, accordingly a Chinaman was sent for. Johnny came looking all smiles and cleanliness with his well-oiled hair, tied-up pig-tail, and short white jacket.

He requested permission to measure the "Mem Sahib's" foot, which he did by untwisting his pig-tail, and measuring with that. In spite of being extremely sensitive with regard to hurting the feelings of one's dependents, we fairly broke down, and had a hearty laugh, which time re-echoes.

I determined one morning to take a short stroll, and found myself near a huge building used for commissariat stores, guarded by a couple of Sepoys. These quaint figures were very striking to a stranger. They were dressed in red tail-coats (coatees were not then invented), black trousers, sandals, and the queerest head-dress you ever saw, something like an inverted black chimney-pot with a knob at the top of it. They looked just like wooden toy soldiers, in their tight-fitting regimentals.

Whilst contemplating these figures, a portion of a European regiment just landed were marching past to their barracks. The scene was most comical. *John Bull* in regimentals could not withstand the ludicrousness of the sight, and one universal peal of laughter swept the ranks. "*I say Bill*" (said one), "*do you call that 'ere a sodger ?*"

I could not resist joining in the merriment, and went home thinking; and yet that toy figure can fight, and fight well too. Let us pay a visit to the China Bazār, a wonderful emporium of every description of merchandize under the sun. It is a large district divided into streets, with very lofty houses on either side; each street is assigned to some particular trade. Thus the iron-smiths have possession of one street; basket-makers of another; milliners a third; glass and crockery ware a fourth.

Suppose yourself in your palkee or palanquin, the bearers carrying you along with their usual chant of "Ho! Hum! Bearer:

CHAR ANNA PIÇA," &c., &c.; and as you approach the scene of action, a black fellow pushes into your hands, say, a case containing a pair of razors. " *E very good razor, saab.*" "Thank you, don't want," is the reply. " *E very cheap, saab, plenty cheap, only seven rupee.*" "Don't want," grumbles John Bull. " *What saab give?*" "Take away." " *E very cheap, saab. There, take three rupee.*" "Take away," sounds from the palkee. " *Saab, one rupee give.*"

In sheer exhaustion the one rupee is given, and you are free from your tormentor for a time; and you have got one of the latest luxuries of the nineteenth century, a shilling razor imported from Birmingham into the glorious East.

The time for proceeding on our journey had now arrived, and we took passage on board the East India Company's steamer *Fire Queen.*

We had for so small a vessel a pretty spacious stern cabin. But who shall describe the difficulties of feeling philosophical and unshuddering, with cockroaches an inch and

a half long running over and around you!
No need of the warning of the African proverb, " *Unless your stomach be strong, do not
eat cockroaches.*" All these vessels, which
never leave the tropics, abound with them ;
and sometimes add to these creeping things
innumerable a little fiery red stinging
ant.

One day I had just completed my toilet
for dinner when the bell rang, and I
hastily took up my hair-brush ; in an instant,
all over, all through my hair, all over my
neck and down to my shoulders, these little
pests were swarming and stinging most
furiously. I had to plunge my head and
neck into water, and certainly I was very
late for dinner. (Moral. When coasting in
Indian vessels, look into your shoes for cockroaches, and at your hair-brush for the fiery
little ant described.)

About a week brought us to the mouth of
the Irawadi, and to Rangoon. The banks of
the river presented rather a Mark Tapley
appearance to us. There was one conspicuously ugly brick structure, a rarity in

Rangoon, occupied as a store by a person rejoicing in the name of Jones and Co.

It was a very useful establishment, and not unlike what an American or colonial store might be. You wandered round a large, counterless room, fitted in the centre with glazed cases containing the more perishable articles of commerce. You stumbled midst frying-pans and saddles, children's toys and tinned meats, wheelbarrows, hoes, and old furniture left on commission sale.

There was no other brick building in existence in Rangoon, with the exception of the General's house in course of construction. At the riverside there was an excellent wooden house belonging to the master attendant. The owner was a pleasant and agreeable man, who from his striking resemblance to Punch, without the hump, enjoyed that soubriquet.

The house was not altogether an unfit abode for such an imaginary personage. You had only to remove the curtains of Punch's domicile, elongate the structure, and you had the house built on piles, presented to your view. It was raised about eight or ten feet from the ground, and built of planks, the roof being formed of bamboos with cadjans or palm-leaves, fastened to narrow strips of bamboo, overlapping each other.

The wood-work had been thoroughly satu-

KAMPTEE BUNGALOW.

rated with earth oil (*petroleum*) to keep away the attacks of white ants. A few months after landing I saw this house burnt to the ground in a quarter of an hour or thereabouts.

Running along the river bank there was a collection of mud-brick houses, inhabited by Chinamen, who had endeavoured in one or

two instances to ornament their frontages
with huge China tiles. Johnny was very
friendly, and always with his cup of tea gave
the European a smiling welcome, midst his
curious dragon-shaped wares and pretty
china.

Opposite to the shops, and on the edge
of the river, were a series of sheds leaf-
thatched, under which the native population
held their bazar. The usual articles of con-
sumption, such as rice, ghee, or clarified
butter, grain, chillies, vegetables, &c., were
here sold, and last but by no means least in its
obtrusiveness, was the shed containing the
GNAPEE. Do you know what GNAPEE is? It
is the most odorous of relishes, relishes I
mean, for the native population. It may be
termed the country " caviare."

It is composed of prawns, fish fry, com-
pounded with chillies, garlic, and other con-
diments. It may be appetizing, but its odour
is abominable. Nothing but a rapid drive
past, with your nostrils covered up, pre-
vents nausea. It is only comparable to a
cargo of burnt rice, the odour of which I

once experienced on the banks of the
Hoogly.

Such was the appearance Rangoon presented, on the banks of the river Irawadi,
many years ago. And yet there was one
object majestically towering over all in the
background.

The Shwe-Dagon pagoda rose magnificently
from the summit of a scarped hill to a great
height. It is a most elegantly bell-shaped
structure of solid brick, covered with gold leaf.
Its apex is surmounted with a circular H'Tee,
or umbrella, a perforated network of metal.

Pendant from this are said to be 600 silver
bells, twenty of pinchbeck, and fifteen of
gold, and with every breath of wind you hear
their silvery music.

The estimated height of this wonderful
monument consecrated to religion, and which
it has attained by successive additions, is
321 feet. It is placed in the centre of a
plateau, which you reach, from the road
approaching it, by an innumerable succession
of steps, I should think a quarter of a mile
in length, bounded on each side by a parapet,

representing a crocodile or some other reptile, throughout its entire length.

These steps are broken at intervals with a square platform over which is erected a species of lych-gate. The timber used as supports is of fine proportion, and for the most part coloured red, with much elaborate carving at the eaves.

The terrace upon which the pagoda stands, encircled with a number of smaller pagodas, all of them of more or less beauty of form, is about 900 feet long, and nearly 700 feet broad. Each smaller pagoda has its H'Tee together with a tall red flagstaff and streamer floating from it.

" The pagoda itself is the object of worship, as containing eight of Guadama's hairs, and some memorials of preceding Buddhas. Lofty trees and leaf-thatched buildings are interspersed with the smaller pagodas, and these contain images of Guadama, a colossal sitting statue of mild appearance with closed eyes. The natives affirm that when Guadama's eyes open, the world will come to an end. They address their prayers alternately with the puff of smoke from their cigar, an action they do not consider in the least irreverent to GUADAMA. Not that he can hear, for he is said to have attained NIRWANA, but the fact of worshipping him is considered to lead to happy births, and ultimately to NIRWANA itself. And so the memory of Guadama comes by Buddhists to be adored."

It is now time, however, that we reached cantonment and our home. We got into a gharrie, a vehicle I have already described, drawn by a fine Pegu pony.

Our charioteer was a wild-looking boy, with a Mongolian type of face. He had not expended much upon clothing, and his turban consisted of a twisted red rag which he managed in some inscrutable manner to interlace with his black hair. He was, however, swift of foot, and ran at the head of the pony. Away we went, helter-skelter, steadying ourselves as best we could, with no little fear as to the result of the journey, until we safely reached our house, constructed of wooden planks, and like its neighbours raised a few feet from the ground on piles.

CHAPTER III.

Duties of chaplains—Modes of visiting out-stations—
Visit to Pegu—Creek adventures—Fire-fly—Mosquitoes, their use—Visiting Burmese villages—
Elegant pagoda—Pegu—Tiger-trap—Narrow escape—Pooay, or Burmese play—English drama in
1587—Native orchestra.

" There is an insect, that, when evening comes,
Small tho' he be, and scarce distinguishable,
Like evening clad in soberest livery,
Unsheaths his wings, and thro' the woods and glades
Scatters a marvellous splendour.   On he wheels,
Blazing by fits as from excess of joy ;
Each gush of light a gush of ecstasy ;
Nor unaccompanied : thousands that fling
A radiance all their own, not of the day ;
Thousands as bright as he, from dusk till dawn,
Soaring, descending.
                                        ROGERS.

WE will commence this chapter by describing
the duties of Indian chaplains.   Unlike military chaplains, who are subject more or less
to the colonel of the regiment to which they
are attached, the Indian chaplain is sub-

ordinated only to his bishop and the government of the Presidency to which he belongs. His services are at the disposal of civil and military alike, in whatsoever station he may be placed. If the station is a large one, there will be two or more chaplains, each with his own church and district assigned him. The churches are built, kept in repair, and furnished by Government, and where there are troops a certain monthly sum allowed for servants, such as clerk, sexton, and peons, or messengers.

Primarily the chaplain has to attend to the troops, visit their different hospitals and barracks, instruct in their schools, and attend the cemetery morning and evening for burials.

The outside or non-military community have also to be attended to, with their schools, hospitals, dispensaries, orphanages, and other institutions.

At certain seasons, out-stations with or without military detachments, and varying from ten to two hundred miles distant, have to be visited.

To each chaplaincy is attached two " Lay

Trustees," or " churchwardens," who, in the
absence of the chaplain, read prayers, and are
bound to notify any irregularity on the part
of the chaplain, and to take care of all
Government church property.

Out of a long course of years it has only
been my misfortune once to have trustees of
the " aggrieved parishioner " type.

In Burmah there were three out-stations to
visit—Pegu, Bassein, and Henzadah. The
Government gives a liberal travelling allow-
ance. The travelling is sufficiently easy by
water, but excessively tiring in up-country
stations by land. I shall describe the different modes of travelling as my history
proceeds. That in Burmah was exceedingly
interesting, offering objects of the deepest
value to any one possessing the tastes of an
antiquarian or naturalist.

Shortly after assuming charge of Rangoon,
I had to start for Pegu and Bassein. I took
advantage of a Government steamer. The
captain was an adventurous spirit, and determined to proceed by some hitherto un-
explored creeks. The journey was full of

interest, anchoring a little before sunset each day, as sandbanks and other obstructions obliged us to navigate by sight alone.

I shall not easily forget the first night we spent in the creeks. We were not more than twenty or twenty-five yards from either bank, thickly clothed with dense jungle and vegetation, splendid teak rising super-eminent.

The atmosphere seemed literally alive with fire-flies.

" But wherefore all night long shine these ? for whom
This gorgeous sight, when sleep hath shut all eyes? "

" It is an insect of very diminutive size, emitting a bright and sparkling light, flitting about and visible at some distance. The substance which emits the light is situated in the extremity of the insect's body, and which appears by daylight and after death as white as wax."

All the undergrowth jungle seemed to be " showers of fire," as Southey calls them, alternately emitting and withdrawing, as if by concerted impulse, their gorgeous colouring of the landscape.

It was as if we were placed between walls of softened fire on the right hand and on the left.

After six p.m. our tormentors, the mosquitoes, frequently compelled us to retire to our berths, and take refuge under the mosquito net curtain. If the vessel was in a tolerably airy position we had a little peace, but on our first night we had not a breath of air stirring. I was forced soon to retire with itching face, wrists, and ankles. My curtains, which were white, looked like black crape, so thickly encrusted were they with these insects. My *boy*, the name for my body-servant, held in his hands a chowrie, i.e. a stick, about a foot long, with horsehair or dried grass attached to its extremity, with which he kept these insects at bay, whilst I undressed and dived into my berth. It is with a sigh of relief you find yourself under the curtains, but woe betide you, if when at an earlier hour, your servant puts them down, he inadvertently leaves any of the enemy in the camp. It is a case not of turn round, but turn out.

A residence of some years in India renders you a little pachydermatous, as the blood gets thinner, but they never cease to annoy; and no country is so good as Burmah for a first seasoning.

The warmth and humidity of the climate no doubt tends to the production of so much insect life, and to that of the mosquito in particular. In no location can the "elephant mosquito," as it is called, be found, in its livery of black with white stripes, in greater perfection.

Mr. Bishop, in his interesting book, "Four Months in a Sneak Box," gives so curious an account of this insect, that at the risk even of wearying my reader's patience, I shall not hesitate to quote from his pages.

"The vices and virtues of the mosquito may be summed up in a few words, always remembering that it is the female and not the male to whom humanity is indebted for lessons of patience.

"The female mosquito deposits about 300 eggs, nearly the shape of a grain of wheat, arranging and glueing them perpendicularly side by side until the whole resembles a solid canoe-like body, which floats about on the surface of the water.

"Press this little boat of eggs deep into the water, and its buoyancy causes it to rise immediately to the surface, where it maintains its true position of a well-ballasted craft, right side up.

"The warmth of the sun, tempered with the moisture of the water, soon hatches the egg, and the larvas, as wigglers or wrigglers, descend to the bottom of the quiet pool, and feed upon the decaying vegetable matter.

"It moves actively through the stagnant water in its passage to the surface, aerifying it and at the same time doing faithfully its work as scavenger by consuming vegetable germs and putrefying matter.

"Professor G. Sanborn and other leading American entomologists assert that the mosquito saves from twenty-five to forty per cent. in a death list among those who are exposed to malarial influences.

"With malaria, the curse of large districts

in the United States, sowing its evil seeds broadcast in our land, and daily closing its iron grasp upon its victims, who could wish for the extermination of so useful an insect as the mosquito?

"When the larva reaches the surface of the water, it inhales, through a delicate tube at the lower end of its body, all the air necessary for its respiration.

"Having lived three or four weeks in the water, during which time it has entered the pupa state, the original skin is cast off, and the insect is transformed into a different and more perfect state.

"A few days later, the epidermis of the pupa falls off, and floats upon the water, and upon this light raft the insect dries its body in the warm rays of the sun; its damp and heavy form grows lighter and more ethereal; it slowly spreads its delicate wings to dry, and soon rises into the clear ether, a perfected being.

"The male mosquitoes retire to the woods and lead an indolent, harmless life among the flowers and damp leaves.

" They are not provided with a lancet, and consequently do not feed upon blood, but suck up moisture through the little tubes nature has given them for that purpose.

" They are a quiet, well-behaved race, and do not even sing; both the music and the sting being reserved for the other sex.

" They rarely enter the abodes of man, and may be easily identified by their heavy feathery antennæ and long maxillary palpi.

" Unfortunately for mankind the female mosquito possesses a most elaborate instrument of torture. She first warns us of her presence by the buzzing sound we know so well, and then settling upon her victim, thrusts into the quivering flesh five sharp organs, one of which is a delicate lancet.

" These organs taken in one mass are called the beak or bill of the insect.

" A writer says;—'The bill has a blunt fork at the end, and is apparently grooved.

Working through the groove, and projecting from the centre of the angle of the fork, is a lance of perfect form, sharpened with a fine bevel.

" ' Beside it the most perfect lance looks like a hand-saw.

" ' On either side of this lance two saws are arranged, with the points fine and sharp, and the teeth well defined and keen.

" ' The backs of the saws play against the lance. When the mosquito alights, with its peculiar hum, it thrusts its keen lance, and then enlarges the aperture with the two saws, which play beside the lance, until the forked bill with its capillary arrangement for pumping blood can be inserted.

" ' The sawing process is what grates upon the nerves of the victim, and causes him to strike wildly at the sawyer.

" ' The irritation of the mosquito's bite is undoubtedly owing to these saws. It is to be hoped that the mosquito keeps her surgical instruments clean, otherwise it might be a means of propagating blood disease.' "

As we generally anchored between four and five p.m., I took the opportunity with one of the steamer officers, who could speak Burmese, of visiting some of the villages on the banks of the creek. We were always very affably received. Many of them had never before seen a European, but our appearance never seemed to excite terror as in many out-of-the-way places in India I had known it to do.

Du Chaillu relates that in an interior African village nothing excited terror more than such an appearance, the women and children running for their lives.

The natives simply seemed surprised, turned up the cuffs of my coat, and rubbed me to see if I was painted, and examined my hair with much curiosity.

The villages I visited seemed to be clean and nicely kept.

The kyoung, or monastery, was the central structure of the village, and a very picturesque one too, with its dormer-like projections, and the exquisite carvings of its eaves.

It is a universal custom for the people to send their children to these institutions to be instructed by the priests; sometimes merely to learn to read and write, and sometimes for years.

ELEGANT PAGODA.

Hence the children grow up with a respect for their religion and their priests, as religious books are placed in their hands as soon as they are capable of reading them.

After a few days' travel we arrived at Pegu. The most striking object here was its elegant tapering pagoda. It had a good deal of

glazed pottery inserted into it, of what antiquity it is impossible to say. These structures are for the most part built of solid
brick, with only a small chamber in the
interior, in which are placed relics and innumerable numbers of small idols, made of
dammer and coated with silver, of Guadama.

Pegu we found to be almost a jungle, the
rainfall very heavy, and evidences of abundance of tigers. Outside a bungalow I saw
a tiger-trap. It had the appearance of a
huge rat-trap, divided into two portions, one
for the reception of the bleating goat, and
the other for the tiger, not giving him room
to turn, which I am enabled to represent
through the kindness of my publishers.

Speaking of travelling in the creeks, I
once witnessed in my civil hospital at Rangoon a most interesting medical case and
cure.

The subject was a native, who must have
been of most temperate habits, or he never
could have survived the shock his system
sustained.

A TIGER TRAP.

Page 60.

He was poling a boat, laden with chickens for the market, when suddenly a tiger sprang from the bank into the middle of the boat. His companion escaped by diving, but the patient in the same act got clawed by the tiger, the epidermis being literally torn down from the nape of the neck like a *strip of wall paper.*

I saw him when first admitted, and when cured, and I think the name of the surgeon who proved his skill was Dr. Dickenson.

I fear our beer or cider-drinking agriculturalist would have stood a small chance of life under such circumstances !

I had now visited my people, held service, and performed all the necessary offices required of me, and the steamer was to be in readiness for the morrow. But there is one more scene to be described which I witnessed.

The Burmese celebrate with much ceremony in November the Incarnation of Guadama, and there was to be a grand " Pooay," or theatrical representation.

" The preparations necessary are of a very

simple character. A cleared space, a framework of bamboos stuck in the ground, over
which, as protection, mats are fastened.

" To a central bamboo branches of trees
are tied, or a branch of a tree brought in
from the jungle and planted in the ground,
at once represents the set scene of every
pooay, a forest.

" An old chair, minus a leg or an arm,
and a bench serve as thrones for rival
monarchs."

The Burmese act themselves, or else use
dolls pulled by wires, a species of Fantoccini,
in fact marionettes, behind a piece of white
cloth. The spectators squat elbow on knee
in front and around, smoking a green cheroot,
with an extra one in the lobe of the ear, as
a reserve, men, women, and children all
enjoying the same luxury.

They will sit for hours enjoying immensely
the weak jokes oft repeated *ad nauseam*, and
seemingly without any palling on the taste
of the audience.

In General Flytche's book on " Burmah
Past and Present," occurs the following

description of a Burmese play, which may supplement anything wanting in that I have given.

He writes :—" It is a strange and curious sight to see the large crowds of Burmese assembled for the night to witness the performance of a pooay, or play, and the delight and perfect good order which they manifest.

" Their attention appears wholly absorbed by the performance, and the sympathy shown for distressed virtue, and rattling peals of laughter caused by the comic parts of the play are very natural.

" The stage accompaniments are rude and simple.

" A structure of bamboos supporting a roof of trellis-work, lightly thatched with grass, and picturesquely draped with bright-coloured silks and cloths, suffice for a theatre.

" The stage is in the centre, and in its midst, around a green bough, unhesitatingly accepted as a substitute for a forest scene, are grouped the footlights, consisting of earthen bowls placed on plantain stems, and fed with petroleum oil.

"Raised bamboo platforms supply the place of boxes, and pit and gallery are represented by the orderly crowd seated close together on the ground. At the back is the orchestra."

Very primitive, or perhaps barbarous, all this; but how about the English drama in the year of grace 1587?

Plays, we are told by Kingsley, were originally acted in the yards of inns. Round the yard ran galleries, roofed in against the weather, the yard being exposed to it.

The common people stood in the yard, on the ground; hence the word of contempt, *groundling*, which lingered until very lately in theatrical *argot*.

In Japan theatres are called " Turf places," because the first performances were held on grass-plots.

Afterwards, we are told, they had boxes or rooms of which the tenant kept the key.

The stage had a gallery behind, which was found useful in representing city walls, &c.,

and there were double or treble rows of curtains by which means the "Player's Play,"
as in Hamlet, could be represented.

At the time of Maclure it is further stated
there was little or no movable scenery, and
the simple old device of hanging up a board
with the name of a locality painted on it,
called "the title," was still resorted to.

But what is a theatrical representation
without music?

It is not wanting here, for at the back, at
the pooay, is the orchestra. There are
amongst them two prominent figures, each
sitting in a circle of carved wood, about
eighteen inches in depth, and each presiding
over his own especial department.

The first, over the drums, which are
wooden or earthenware, stretched over with
skin, and fastened to the inner side of the
circle.

On one side of the player, who sits in the
centre, is a lump of damp sand. With this
he modulates the tones with one hand,
increasing or diminishing the quantity placed
on the skin of the drum, and with the other

F

dexterously eliciting the "*harmonious dis-cord.*"

The second notable personage presides over the cymbals, the lower half of which are fixed like the drums, two upper halves he holds in his hands, with which he strikes the lower.

Burton, in his African travels, speaks of bamboos used *à la castanet.*

He says, " A favourite instrument is a clapper, made of two bamboos some five feet long, and thick as capstan-bars—it is truly the castanet *en grand.*"

The Burmese use the bamboo after a similar manner, but not larger than five or six inches in diameter, and two feet in length, split to within six inches of the end, the vibrating portions being sharply clapped together.

In addition to these were trumpets of various sizes, all creating. a wild, but not altogether inharmonious din.

" *O cara, cara !* silence all that train,
Joy to great *chaos !* let division reign."

CHAPTER IV.

Rangoon—Mode of building houses—Rides—*Bambusa gigantea* and *Bambusa tulda*—Bamboo—Its uses—The dha—Lacquered boxes and mode of lacquering—Home for breakfast—Novel watch-dog—Bantams—Ponies—Tucktoo—A dinner under unpleasant circumstances—Native burglar—Attack by Dacoits—"Sufficient unto the day is the evil thereof"—Rainy season—Burmese character—Instances of cruelty—Excruciating tortures.

"Knowledge makes knowledge as money makes money, nor ever perhaps so fast as on a journey."

ROGERS.

"To a man of intelligence and education there is no glory in a constant residence: therefore quit thy native place and go abroad."

LANE.

THE steamer is off, and we are on our way back to headquarters.

The troops in Rangoon consisted of a

F 2

European regiment, some native regiments and artillery, officered by Europeans.

We had no church, properly speaking, but service was held in a disused phöngyee or priest's house.

The early morning ride towards the end of the year was very pleasant: throughout the year, however, it was very hot in the middle of the day, but the nights were invariably cool, and you could sleep well.

Passing through the cantonment, a stranger would be puzzled at the sight of a number of bamboos stuck upright in the ground; but should he be repassing on the morrow, he would see at about four or five feet from the ground plaited bamboo mats, forming a flooring and walls to the future habitation.

Then some wooden doors and windows followed by bamboo poles again to support the light cadjan roofing. The roof itself being protected from the wind by a network of thin split bamboo.

Not a nail was there in the whole habitation, every part being securely tied with rattan (*calamus*) soaked and made into string.

The manner in which the houses are raised from the ground is shown in the illustration which depicts an old phöngyee house used at this time as a church.

PHÖNGYEE HOUSE USED AS A CHURCH.

We had the most charming rides all round Rangoon. The soil was sandy, and we had miles and miles of well-sheltered spaces for our canter.

Pine-apples grew in luxuriant abundance; a tart and luscious grape of golden colour festooned the trees; orchids, ferns and creepers delighted the eye on every side, but nothing was so grand and beautiful as the over-arching and graceful bamboo.

The *Bambusa gigantea* attains a diameter of eight inches in Pegu, but the most wonderful species is *Bambusa tulda*, this attains its full height of seventy feet in a single month, i.e. at the average an inch in an hour.

Mr. Robinson says of the Bamboo, " He is an old man who can say, 'I have seen the bamboo flower twice,' for the bamboo flowers but once in thirty years, and when it has flowered it dies."

Innumerable are the uses to which the bamboo is put.

They construct their houses with it. Baskets, boxes, masts, spear-handles, sticks, water-buckets, cages, traps and so on *ad infinitum.*

It is in fact, to the Burman, what the cocoa-nut tree is to the East Indian.

The instrument with which the bamboo is cut down and manufactured into the most beautiful of shapes in the form of baskets, is the Dha.

This weapon is about three feet long and an inch and a half in breadth, fixed in a handle, with a slight uniform curve from end to end. They fell trees with it, or kill animals *or their enemies*, and also execute the finest basket-work.

They cut the bamboo into the very thinnest strips with it, plait, and then lacquer it over, rendering the object impervious to heat or damp.

The manner in which the boxes and cups are lacquered is very interesting.

Mr. Sanderson writes on this subject thus: "The principal occupation of some of the Burmese villagers is the manufacture of lacquered boxes.

" First, a box in the shape required of fine bamboo basket-work; this is dipped in *thitsee* (wood oil), and buried for five or six days, or until the lacquer is properly set on the bamboo.

" Again dipped and buried, and for a third time the process is repeated.

" The frame is thus covered with a good coating of the lacquer. On this is traced the pattern which it is intended to produce in red tracing, say.

" The red pigment is then rubbed over the whole, but bites where the tracing has been made only.

" After being allowed to remain a few days, the superfluous red pigment is rubbed off.

" There is then traced out the pattern which it may be intended to produce in yellow, and the above process is repeated with yellow pigment, and so, until all the tracing is done and coloured.

" The whole is then put on a lathe and polished with fine charcoal. The pattern is traced by a little iron style and by the eye entirely."

We will now suppose ourselves entering our compound (or house premises), after our ride.

We have one of the best of watchers, who lives underneath the house, in the shape of a *Chinese pig.* No sooner does any visitor approach, than out he rushes with innumerable grunts announcing the arrival.

And who is that pretty little lady and gentleman so composedly perched on the verandah rail?

It is a veritable Burmese bantam and his spouse. See how his minute framework quivers as he essays to deliver himself of his crow.

And Jenny has just laid an egg in my wife's Swiss hat, an egg not much larger than that of a dove.

"Are they feathered?" asks a connoisseur. Yes, down to the very tips of their dainty little toes.

Our handsome Pegu ponies have been led away to the stable, on whose virtues I shall not descant, save that they can climb anywhere, as one hears nothing more frequently discussed at mess than their merits.

Horses do not thrive in Burmah, as they are apt to get paralyzed in the loins, hence ponies are in great request.

We will go into the drawing-room, but what is that noise to which one has become quite accustomed?

Distinct enough, *Tuck—too*. Well, I have

a fine specimen in spirits, so we need not
disturb him, as he clings to our wooden
planked ceiling.   He is a foot long, and
learned men, I am told, call him *Tachy-
dromus sex-lineatus*.

There are some smaller ones, too, which
have their abode under the dining-room table,
and which come up for the crumbs at dinner-
time, usually called, I think, Gecko, or *Hœmi-
dactylus coclei*. Nothing can be more amusing
than to watch their actions on the wall.
Still, as if carved in wood for a moment, a
closer inspection reveals their eyes prying
round with dilated orbits to catch sight of
their prey; and then all at once a dart and a
capture, at any angle, for the suckers with
which Nature has provided its feet, enables
it to keep its balance in any position.
" Honest creatures who," as Bulwer says,
" openly confess that they live on flies."

Some of these smaller fry I have seen fall
on a fair neighbour's neck and leave an ugly
red mark afterwards.

Charming land ! Yes, come and enjoy a
dinner with me on a close sultry evening,

without a breath of air stirring, when I have got my mosquito room ready.

But try and dine on such an evening without this artificial aid, and get for your pains a flight of green bugs, poisoning your soup and infecting everything with their abominable stench.

These are some of the luxuries of the East. There are more to narrate, which this history will unfold.

I have already spoken of the plaited bamboo matting and of the expert use the Burmans make of their dha.

An engineer friend of mine told me the following tale :—

He lived in one of these altogether bamboo habitations, and had charge of the cash-chest of his department.

It was about two a.m. (the time when the natives consider that the Europeans sleep most soundly), that he was awakened by feeling something cold on his ankle. Fearing that it was a snake, without moving, he opened his eyes to survey the position.

It had been the hand of a native who was

in the room, and who thought him to be fast asleep.

The house was shut up, all the doors closed, and the burglar had got in by cutting with his dha a hole in the bamboo flooring.

In a second he made a spring from his bed, seized a chair, with which he tried to pin the man down. He failed in this, and endeavoured to seize him, but being oiled—a common custom with them when on such expeditions—the burglar escaped.

I had, some months afterwards in Rangoon, a somewhat similar encounter, with the exception that there were several men, and and they failed to effect an entrance into my bungalow.

It was on this wise :—

We had been dining out, and had not returned until nearly twelve p.m., a late hour for India. I was consequently restless, and about two a.m. was awakened by something falling upon the wooden floor near the Venetian window.

I said to my wife, "What is that?" and she replied, "*Only my scissors!*" The ludicrousness of the answer immediately aroused me.

I got up, and found the muslin curtain pushed inwards. One of the panes of glass was partly broken; and in trying to put the hand in to pull down the bolt, the Dacoit had broken more of the glass.

There were three or four of these men, who had come down the river, landed at the bottom of my compound, and were desirous of not returning empty-handed.

Our night-light was burning on the dressing-room table, where lay our watches and my wife's bracelets, a glittering prize.

I saw the men in the verandah smoking their cheroots. I immediately rushed into the next room, with more impetuosity than wisdom, for had it not been empty I should to a certainty have been cut down with a dha.

I then called up my butler, and sent him to the mess-house opposite for the sentinel. Meantime the men, alarmed, decamped across my pretty balsam beds.

The guard came, inspected the premises,

and departed; whilst we, unable to sleep and thankful for our escape, wished for daybreak.

The Burman is constitutionally very strong, he can endure great fatigue, and live almost entirely on the produce of the forest, hence his only care is for the present.

If he were tolerably industrious and would work for two days in the week, he would have no difficulty in supporting himself for the remaining five days.

One day, after a sudden storm of wind which had carried off a portion of my roof, I sent for some men to repair it.

Half a dozen came, and were to receive eight annas each per diem, that is, one shilling for their hire. This was very good payment, as the same amount of labour could be obtained in India for threepence.

Half the day had passed away, and little progress had been made. They had occupied their time chiefly in smoking and joking— one uttered a joke, which was repeated half a dozen times over and as continually received with peals of laughter.

I was thinking of night-time and its pro-
bable fall of rain, having had to walk about
my drawing-room with an umbrella, and so
sent my servant to hurry them. They were
offended, and walked off unpaid, leaving me
in no very comfortable frame of mind. I,
learnt, however, to be more patient and en-
during midst these tattooed gentry.

Nearly every male is tattooed from the
waist to the knees with black or blue pigment, in figures of lions, tigers, &c., on a
groundwork of fine tracery. The operation
for it commences at the age of six years, and
is done gradually until completed, the process
extending sometimes over many years.

They are a fine robust race, wear their
hair tied in a knot on the top of the head,
and wound round or intertwined with it is a
fine piece of muslin; a jacket of cotton, a
potso of bright silk or cotton wound round
the waist, extending to the ankles and thrown
over their shoulder, has been aptly described
as forming their dress.

They are a lively and impulsive race, and
moreover, irascible and cruel.

I will give one instance of the latter quality which came under my own observation.

I was called one day to visit a dying soldier. The poor fellow had been sentry over some commissariat stores situated some distance from the cantonment.

During the night he had been attacked and struck down from behind. He presented a lamentable spectacle, his face appeared twice its ordinary size, the features being rendered almost indistinguishable; he had been beaten with a blunt bamboo. He expired very shortly after I had visited him.

That they are cruel, like most barbarous nations, I think admits of no doubt, and did one exist, the following extract will suffice to set that question at rest.

In the memoirs of the famous Salim Jahanjir, the Moghul emperor, authenticated by himself, he says, " To strengthen and confirm my rule I directed that a double row of stakes should be set up, from the garden to the city, and that the rebels and others who had taken part in the revolt should be impaled thereon, and thus receive their deserts in this most excruciating punishment."

Again he says, "Than this there cannot exist a more excruciating punishment, since the wretches exposed frequently linger a long time in the most agonizing torture before the hand of death relieves them.

"The process consisted of lightly poising the victim over a sharp stake, in such a manner that, by wriggling in the contortions of his agony, he should gradually impale himself."

Such passages forcibly remind one of Pliny's celebrated letter to the Emperor Trajan regarding the sufferings of the early Christians.

CHAPTER V.

Rangoon cantonment—A " festa"—Dress—Phöngyees
and their acolytes—Character—Funeral rites—Football—Buffalo fight—Boat-racing—Monsoon and its
effects—Bishop Wilson and the brigadier—The
bishop's address to soldiers, and departure.

"It is the voice of years that are gone!
  They roll before me with all their deeds."

OSSIAN.

THE appearance of the Rangoon cantonment
only differed from other cantonments in the
look of the houses, with their light leaf
roofs.

It had its cavalry, artillery, and infantry
lines, with the officers' houses grouped near
to each arm of the service. The roads here
and there were dotted about with pagodas,
and a grotesque figure or two of huge dimensions and Egyptian character.

The pagodas had all been looted, that is, the small silver images of Guadama found in them had been stolen. The chief road in the cantonment led to the Shwe-Dagon pagoda, which I have already described. The Pyramids of Egypt strike the beholder with awe and wonder, but the beautiful tapering bell-shape of the Dagon, with its inimitable proportions, whilst making you feel your own insignificance, impresses you with a deep sense of its exquisite beauty.

It was one of the prettiest sights imaginable on a " festa " to see the crowds of men, women, and children, all gaily and brightly dressed, going up to the pagoda to make their offerings. Not less picturesque in the group were the Phöngyees, or priests, in their orange and saffron-coloured satin robes.

The men and women were clothed in their long *potsos* of divers coloured silks. The women bore on their heads brass trays of offerings, sweetmeats, plantains, gold leaf, &c., &c., and a little gum screwed up in a leaf to enable them to stick a leaf on the sacred shrine. They and the girls also adorned their raven-black tresses with fresh flowers of the chumpac or jasmine,—

"So studiously their persons they adorn."

They are much fairer in complexion than the men, and their features more delicate. They have indeed very good features, small hands and feet, and well-proportioned limbs, which the peculiar disposition of the flowing potso enables you to observe.

Their most remarkable ornaments of adornment are their earrings, or rather ear-tubes. These are cylinders of thin gold, one inch and a half in length, and three quarters of an inch in diameter, and into which very frequently a cheroot is thrust; for in Burmah, as on the Vizagapatam coast, men, women, and children all smoke.

In the town it was an interestiug sight to see the Phöngyees marching from stall to stall, to receive the people's offerings for their daily maintenance. They were accompanied by boy acolytes, who carried a large lacquered box, in which the cup of boiled

rice was deposited ; grain, ghee, vegetables,
all alike acceptable.

Bishop Cotton says of them, " They are
a fair average set of priests, doing nothing
to raise their countrymen and turn Burmah
into a real nation, nor particularly active or
self-denying or learned, but maintaining a
decent exterior and conversation according
to their lights.

The Phöngyees do not practise asceticism
at all, they still keep to the rule of mendicancy,
but receive such ample and handsome presents, that this causes them no self-denial.

" It is generally admitted that they are
respected by the laity.

" Guadama, by his destruction of caste,
showed himself a real social reformer, and the
good effects of his teaching are visible here
in Burmah, after he has been dead 2400
years.

" The great moral defect of the system
which he taught, is its almost exclusive
inculcation, or at least extravagant exalta-
tion, of the passive virtues ; its great spiritual
weakness is the entire omission of a per-

sonal God, or any living or conscious Saviour.

Another writer remarks, "In the early morning in all the towns and villages of Burmah are to be seen long files of Phöngyees perambulating the streets at a measured pace, with their alms-bowls slung round their necks, into which people pour food as they pass.

"They are barefooted, and have no covering for the head, which is shaven. In the right hand they carry a large palm-leaf fan which they hold before their face in the presence of women, so that no evil thoughts may enter the mind.

"They are forbidden to ask for food, to look to the right hand or the left, and they may not enter or loiter about the doors of houses. When anything is poured into their bowls, they do not return thanks, but content themselves by saying 'thada, thada,' that is, 'well, well,' and when sufficient has been obtained to appease their hunger they return to the monasteries to eat it.

"Nothing whatever is cooked in the monasteries. Many Burmese consider it a great act of merit to make a vow never to partake of a meal without reserving a portion of it for the Phöngyees."

The Burmans are all Buddhists, and number a quarter of the whole human race. To be a pious Buddhist you must remain, it is said, "unaffected by surrounding objects, deny yourself everything beyond the bare necessaries of life, and consider all things transitory, and productive of unhappiness, and unreal."

Captain Parry, speaking of the Buddhists of China, says, "They are a very degraded lot, and so little respected, that they have become a by-word and term of reproach. They are a miserable imitation of its pure type in Burmah."

All accounts with which I am acquainted give the same character to the Burman Buddhists, that of being the purest type of a strange devotion.

"With regard also to their ultimate conversion to Christianity, they are, without the bigotry of caste, like the Hindoos or Mohammedans."

Bishop Milman, in writing of them, says, "I have hope that the Buddhist will soon become receptive of Christianity . . . . It is the purest and most enlightened form of heathenism, and in Burmah is free from the intermixture of Shivaism, which has mingled with it in Nepal and in Ceylon, and the superstitions of Thibet or China."

A short distance out of the cantonment is a large burial-ground for the natives. It was on this spot I once witnessed the burial of a Phöngyee.

I cannot describe the antecedent preparations and the ceremony itself better than in the words of two of my old friends, General Fytche and Colonel Laurie, men who have both distinguished themselves in arms and literature.

The former writes, "The state of a priest when alive is regarded as one of great sanctity, and their very persons thereby rendered holy. Great honours are therefore paid to their mortal remains. As soon as a priest has expired, his body is opened, the viscera extracted, and the body embalmed, after which the corpse is swathed with bandages of linen, and covered over with a thick coat of varnish.

" It is then placed between two solid pieces of wood, hollowed out for the purpose, and boiling resin poured into the interstices until every crevice is filled. When this is completed, the coffin is gilded, and placed on a platform, under a handsomely decorated canopy in one of the rooms of the monastery or in a separate building erected for the purpose in its vicinity, and there lies in state until preparations are completed for the cremation, which often extend over some months."

Colonel Laurie says, " In general the last rites even where no signs of great wealth is observable, are performed with extravagant splendour.

" The bier of the deceased, raised on high, and enclosed in the model of a Buddhist temple, borne along on the shoulders of some dozens of bearers ; the glaring red and gilt and silvery ornaments of the grotesque machine, to which a grace is given by the white flags and umbrellas attached to it ; the long train of followers, chiefly women, in rear, and Phöngyees in front. Such is a faint outline of the richer Burmese funeral."

He then quotes a funeral seen and described by Lieutenant Cadell, which, from its minute ceremonial description, is well worthy of attention.

"Women and children attended as well as men. Old women were howling in a most disconsolate manner.

"On reaching the burial-ground, the Phöngyees came forward and took up their position on a raised platform at the head of the grave. Before the priests were placed three large dishes of plantains and dried fish. Pieces of wood were put across the grave, and the coffin rested on them. The men then kneeled round the priests, and the women and children formed an outer semicircle. A Phöngyee then repeated a few prayers, to which the men responded. Then a long prayer was said, and while the priest was speaking a man was pouring water slowly on the ground from a small earthenware vessel.

"This finished the ceremony, and the

Phöngyees, having had their provisions carefully collected, departed. The corpse was
then taken from the coffin and buried.
Buddhists, it must be remembered, bury as
well as burn. Pouring the water from the
earthen vessel is to signify the spirit depart-
ing from the body."

In the funeral I witnessed combustibles
were placed about the body, and the whole
completely destroyed by fire. How striking
the contrast of this with a *Christian military
funeral*, when after all the sad feelings evoked
by hearing the " Dead March in Saul " played
by the military band, with its affecting accom-
paniment of arms reversed ; the dead body lies
quietly reposing, and awaiting its last great
awakening. The crowd disperses ; and with
the order " Quick march," a lively and in-
spiriting tune is struck up. Even so, let us
pass away from this " place of a skull," and
see, in this open space adjoining, a game of
football, played by the young men of Burmah.

It is played with a small ball of wicker-
work—very light, with interstices. The
players form a circle, and keep up the ball

with remarkable skill; with knee and foot they send it flying in every direction, as Colonel Laurie says, "as if they were perfect masters in the law of projectiles."

He also mentions their buffalo fights. In these the men sit on the beasts, and rush at each other with tremendous fury. Frequently the horns become interlocked, when a trial of strength ensues, each pushing his adversary as far back as possible. The buffaloes after a stout contest generally become tired of the sport, and not unfrequently scamper away from their tormentors. The buffalo is seldom killed, but the rider not unfrequently is thrown.

Cock-fighting, wrestling, and boat-racing complete the most notable of their games.

The boat-racing is very exciting. Two or more boats on either side, containing twenty to thirty rowers each, all paddling with amazing swiftness, and a man in the centre of each boat, gesticulating, dancing, and encouraging the competitors to win the "laurel wreath" in the form of a whisp of grass suspended from a boat ready for them to grasp, forms a very pretty and amusing scene.

" The glorious garland's held in open show,
　To cheer the lads, and crown the conqueror's brow."

They are very fond of a game of cards, and play a species of chess or draughts, the pieces representing elephants and other animals and men.

In Rangoon there is a heavy and long monsoon, which usually begins even to a certain hour on the 24th of May.

The sun is intensely burning at this time; but throughout the year the nights are cool and sleepable. The excessive damp mildews everything which is not protected from its influence. The lacquered boxes made by the natives are invaluable for preserving your gloves and clothes. If left unprotected, boots become red and spotted, gloves mildewed; paste comes through the covers of your cloth-bound books, and you leave their outsides on the table. To keep things at all in proper order, it is necessary during the monsoon time to keep charcoal burning throughout the house.

The combination of heat and moisture with the hard work incident on cantonment and town duties was pressing too heavily upon me in a climate where the slightest bodily exertion was a great fatigue. Accustomed from my earliest years to be self-helpful, in Burmah I was unable to dispense with the services of what is called a dressing-boy.

I had been without any relaxation or help for thirteen months, and though the troops belonged to the Madras Presidency, ecclesiastically I found myself subject to Bengal.

This brought me into communication with the Indian Metropolitan, good Bishop Wilson, of pious memory. I have already stated that there was no proper church, service being held in a disused Phöngyee house. A site was selected, and the Metropolitan was coming on visitation, and to lay the foundation-stone. The Bishop was to stay with the Brigadier, the general being absent. He was a fine, soldierly man, but held peculiar religious views. I met the Bishop on landing, and went with his lordship to the Brigadier's.

The latter immediately invited me to his hospitable table during the Bishop's stay, for whom I was to act as chaplain extraordinary, as he already had his domestic chaplain with him. We were invited to breakfast with him that day.

When assembled, the Bishop's private chaplain read one of the lessons for the day, which happened to be the sixteenth chapter of the Acts of the Apostles, narrating the conversion of the jailor.

After the chapter had been read the Bishop gave a concise and learned *résumé* of it, and wound up by turning to his soldier host and saying, "*And so you see, Brigadier, the Baptists have not a leg to stand upon.* Let us pray."

Deeply in earnest, the good man poured forth his aspirations, not neglecting to pray by name for all his relatives. This was rather trying to strangers who were not acquainted with them.

His lordship became in his latter days slightly eccentric. He had been in his day a very powerful preacher, and he kindly consented one evening to preach in my town church. This was little better than a hut, but served in those days for me to get the sailors who frequented the place together.

On this occasion many soldiers of the garrison were present, and this is one sentence of his lordship's discourse: " *I love the British soldier. He is a fine, brave, strong, courageous fellow, a lion in the path of his enemy; but* (imitating the act of drinking) *when the liquor goes down, the devil goes down with it.*"

Next came the laying of the foundation-stone of the church.

The troops were paraded on three sides of an extensive square. There was a raised dais in the centre, and the fourth side was set apart for the civilians and families of officers not on duty.

The foundation-stone being laid, a hymn was sung, and then followed an address from the bishop. The ceremony over, the good old man, though infirm in the extreme, with the true courtesy of an English gentleman insisted on seeing my wife home.

The following day was appointed for the bishop's departure. His lordship having requested me to see him on board, which under any circumstances I should have done, he talked long and earnestly with me in his cabin on my work, and then said, "*Now kneel down and receive my blessing.*" Verily the less was blessed of the greater.

He was, as his whole life evinced, at once a bishop and a saint.

CHAPTER VI.

Return to India—Ordered to the Central Provinces—
Akyab—Calcutta—Up the Ganges to Mirzapore—
A grim spectacle on the river—Palkee travelling
—Dâk bungalows—Adventure—Jubbulpore—A fel-
low chaplain—Thugs' Institution—Their industries
—Thuggee and its suppression—Shell-lac—Marble
Rocks—Fakir—A future " minor canon."

" Men and manners I describe."
                                    MARTIAL.

I HAVE previously stated that I had requested
to be removed to my own Presidency. In
reply my bishop had asked to what station I
wished to be appointed. I knew nothing of
the country—all stations were alike to me—
and I replied that I was ready to go where-
ever his lordship was pleased to send me.

I was now ordered to Kamptee, in the
Central Provinces. It was a long journey,
involving a passage first of all to Calcutta, a

month's journeying up the Ganges as far as Mirzapore, and then several hundred miles across country to my station.

The chaplain who was to relieve me having arrived, we started *viá* Akyab to Calcutta in the steamer *Fire Queen*.

We had not been at sea for thirteen months, but having been good sailors, we did not anticipate much inconvenience from so short a trip. But man is stomach. Agreeing thus far with Plato, we may proceed to say the motion was disagreeable, the vessel crowded, and our berth small. We were sick, but not unto death.

The voyage was a very stormy one, and the coast dangerous. Cyclones frequently occur in these parts, in one of which a doctor friend, a few years afterwards, with all hands on board, perished.

The commissariat on board was very indifferent; but having an officer on board accustomed to such emergencies, his private stores, bestowed with liberal hand, left us nothing to complain of. Never had we passed such a miserable Christmas Day—

luggage all over the deck, an *omnium ga-therum* of people delighting in lotteries and foolishness.

We arrived at Akyab—a desolate-looking place, memorable to us as having given us rest, from a restless ocean. The place consisted of a few huts, as usual built on piles, a bazaar, with abundance of fruit and the lacquered bamboo-boxes in abundance, designed to hold betel-leaf, nuts, and chunam. This acrid mixture the natives delight to chew, and no doubt it gives to the women as much pleasure as smoking does to the rougher sex.

Speaking of the *betel* or *areca*-nut, Dr. Hooker, writing about it, says: "The cultivated areca raises its graceful head and feathery crown like an arrow shot from heaven, in luxuriance and beauty above the verdant slopes."

The nut itself is about the size of a cherry, slightly pear-shaped, very hard, and externally not unlike a nutmeg of inferior quality. It is chewed along with the leaf of the betel pepper, and a little quicklime. Mr. Johnston

says that the natives would rather forego
meat and drink than their favourite betel.
It is supposed to cool the mouth, cleanse
the gums, and fasten the teeth. It is really
conducive to health in damp and malarious
districts, especially where the natives live on
spare diet.

After seven days' voyage we arrived at
Calcutta for the second time. We had the
greatest difficulty in procuring lodgings,
every place being filled on account of some
impending races. At last we got settled in
tolerably comfortable quarters in a central
position.

I again visited Bishop's College. I was
much struck with the shifting nature of the
sands in the river Hooghly. Last year the
river was quite deep near the college; this
year a large space of sand intervened between
the river and the bank. The bed of the
river is constantly changing, which makes
navigation very risky, and the guidance of a
pilot for large vessels absolutely necessary.

Vessels of deep draught have to be very
carefully navigated by these able and com-

petent men, for if a vessel even touches she may be endangered or lost.

I saw a good deal of Calcutta this visit. God gave me my first child here, who gladdened my heart for sixteen years, and was then withdrawn in His wise providence, for "*she pleased Him*." Ah! as Southey truly says, "it is a bitter cup; and, as we live on, our friends and our relatives drop through the broken arches of the bridge of life; but *we would fain pass away first!*"

Towards the end of January we again ventured forth on our toilsome journey, and embarked on board the *Lady Thackwell* steamer, to proceed up the Ganges to Mirzapore.

We had a flat, or barge, in tow, whereon all the heavy luggage was placed, as well as merchandise intended for the different ports at which we should stop. It was a pleasant time of rest after the hard work in Burmah. Our *dolce far niente* life was varied by our touching at some station, such as Benares or Dinapore or Patna, where cargo had to be discharged or embarked.

On such occasions the natives brought off their wares for sale, and the scene became very animated and amusing. The European, in spite of his shrewdness, was invariably taken in by his sable brother. The latter lives very much on the principle of a celebrated upholsterer, who was asked, so the tale goes, how he recovered his debts from the petty rajahs—who were supposed to require long credit. He replied that they were the best customers he had, for " I do charge double, and take half in advance."

There was little to vary the monotony of the journey. The scenery for the most part was dreary and featureless in the extreme— a wide expanse of arid shifting sand, on which no building could with safety be constructed, under a glaring sun for hundreds of miles on either side of us.

There seemed abundance of fish of various kinds; and now and then floated by the body of a dead Hindoo, pushed into the sacred river by affectionate friends, on its way to their paradise.

In those days—and I am speaking of the

year of the great mutiny—death was not
unfrequently hastened by relatives, seeing the
end inevitable, thrusting mud into the mouth
and nostrils of the dying subject. I saw on
the banks of the river solitary parties, who
had brought those *in extremis,* to do for them
the last offices of riddance or affection.

A few sticks, with cadjans over them,
sufficed for protection from the sun.

It was a grim spectacle to see the corpse
floating down, with crows and vultures bat-
tening on their loathsome feast. The dark
corpse, and the white blotches where the
epidermis had been torn away, formed a
sickening and revolting sight.

I remember, whilst staying in Garden
Reach, taking an early morning's walk on
the banks of the muddy Hooghly, and seeing
people employed on purpose to thrust off,
with boat-hook, the dead bodies which had
stranded during the night. The custom of
thrusting the bodies into the river has been
forbidden, and the chains of the ships at
anchor relieved of their ghastly burdens.
Far sweeter the boxes manufactured out of

the Jack-tree (*Artocarpus*), and rubbed with sandal-wood oil to represent *real sandal-wood*, by the crafty native, offered to us on our journey up the river.

We reached Mirzapore. Time waits for no man, much less do steamers on their onward passage : we were quickly put on shore, bag and baggage. Having taken my wife and child to the dâk bungalow, I started off to a merchant's stores to purchase palanquins, or, as we called them, palkees, for the land journey of several hundred miles still before us.

That which is one man's loss is another's gain. Persons leaving the country sell their palkees for little or nothing. I was able to get for five pounds a very good palkee, which had originally cost seventy. This was de-signed for the "Mem-Sahib" and the little one. For myself I procured a dhoolie, or frame-work covered with canvas, and very light. Palkees purchased, bearers had to be hired. Four-and-twenty bearers, two *banghy-burdars*, or men to carry two tin boxes each, slung on the ends of a bamboo and carried over the shoulder, and two *mussalchee* men, to carry torches for the night journey.

And now a few words about the dâk bungalow, or rest-houses, of India. There is a bungalow at each large station, containing two or more sets of rooms. These are provided by the Government, who places a servant in charge, who provides, on payment, refreshment for the traveller. To prevent the " rest-house " being converted into a cheap lodging-house, they can be tenanted only for a few hours. A small fee is paid towards the maintenance of the establishment. A table, chairs, bed, crockery, and glass are provided. They take the place of the English wayside inns, without the presence of mine host and hostess.

On leaving, you enter in a book the date of your arrival and departure, the fee you have paid, and make any remarks, in a column provided for the purpose, regarding the state of the bungalow, attention or inattention of the Government servant. In large stations, ample provisions may be obtained, but they are lamentably scarce in less civilized parts. They are placed at different distances; ten, twenty, and even thirty miles apart.

Suppose now that we have made our onward start at 4.30 p.m.; we shall probably get to our halting-place at seven or eight a.m. the following morning. An old stager will always contrive to make an early start—a good principle to go upon in life—and thence, in spite of all accidents, he has a chance of arriving at his destination ere the sun gets uncomfortably warm.

He will always be, waking or sleeping, more or less on the *qui-vive*, for, if not, when master is asleep the bearers will stop and have a smoke; for the native holds with Molière, " *Qui vit sans tabac, n'est pas digne de vivre,*" and he will find himself late and wearied at the next stage.

Within a quarter of a mile of the bungalow, your bearers, poor fellows, will quicken their pace, renew their song, making all the noise they possibly can with their metallic voices, and arrive, oft-times, jaded and footsore, glad at the prospect of a few hours' rest. The butler will be seen rushing madly about, opening doors and windows, and coming to greet you with becoming salaam.

You roll yourself out of your palkee, tell him to get breakfast " plenty quick," and make tracks for the life-giving bath ere the day's campaign commences.

" Well, butler, what have you got for breakfast ? "

" Please, master, what want ? Plenty things got."

If you are fortunate, the " plenty things " eventuate in a chop of goat or mutton, a tough old fowl curried, some minutely small eggs, and chuppattees, a thin cake of dough, which takes hours to digest.

Of course you have your own stores of tea and coffee. You have now had your bath and your breakfast, possibly a whiff such as helped the poor bearers on their toilsome way, when, in spite of all alertness, you had a temporary snooze.

Mamma has had the baby to attend to, whose wants have been supplied with un-wearying devotion ; the " Lessons of the Day " have been read ; and you are thrust upon your own private stock of literature to beguile the time for the next three or four hours.

It is rather up-hill work. The thermometer at 90°; the glare outside unabated; the house shut up; the monotonous punkah *swing! swing! swing!* the unwearied mosquitoes; and the *very white* whitewashed walls of the *very square* square room, all tend to numb the faculties, and make you tire of the "Dâk Bungalow Regulations" which adorn the walls of the hospitium.

But even so, time passes away. It is enlivened also by certain raids made by the butler, who comes for payment for the bearers, and money for the torch-men.

There is also the re-packing; much of your comfort or discomfort for the following day will depend upon the manner in which this is carried out. Clothes will be easily disposed of in your palkee, whilst the eatables must be so arranged as to avoid collision, if possible.

The *banghy-burdars* have an alacrity in putting down their burdens with a bang, whereby tea and sardines, jam and coffee, marmalade and anchovies, are apt to get confused; so arrange your *pittaras*, as your tin cases are called, with loving care.

You are now about to re-enter your palkee, and find yourself surrounded with a crowd of expectants, all desiring *baksheesh* for some imaginary kind office, or gathered together to have a last peep at the *mem-sahib* and her little *missie baba*. It is not perhaps astonishing, under these circumstances, that the bag of rupees provided for the journey grows beautifully less and less.

One night we were travelling along, when about twelve o'clock I awakened, to find both palkees on the ground and the bearers afar off, regaling themselves with whiffs out of their hubble-bubbles, though they declared they were taking *khana*, i.e. a meal.

It is a word never out of the night or day-dream of a native. If a beggar salutes you, it is with the request that you will give him pice for his *khana*. If a servant is late, he has been to his *khana*. If a man is absent from the stables, he is getting *khana.* They seem never to be occupied with anything else. Pardon this digression; it reminds me of what Mr. Shiel says of engaging a native servant.

Three stages have to be passed through. Stage one, he gets fever. Stage two, his mother or his grandmother dies. Stage three, his sister gets married. After that, and he has had his *khana,* he will begin to consider the propriety of attending to his master's wants.

The excuse then of *khana* was the excuse of the day, had been so for generations, and will be so *in sæcula sæculorum.*

To continue: I know not how long they had been regaling themselves, but after walking about with my wife in a nasty tigerish-looking district, and suggesting that the palkee wherein was the cynosure of all her hopes might be attacked, she urged me to rouse up the men.

With gentle persuasion, and a mild push to this man and a help to another, I succeeded in rendering them so thoroughly uncomfortable that they at last put their necks to the yoke, or rather their shoulders to the pole, and on we went.

Looking back on this very small adventure, I often wonder we escaped so well. The men were all disaffected, and we were on the eve of the Mutiny.

We learnt afterwards, from a doctor who travelled the same route, that at that lonely spot all his bearers had forsaken him. Fortunately he had an excellent servant with him yclept a *boy*, from the Hindustani, and signifying brother, who found a village, and procured some coolies to supply the place of the defaulting bearers. The poor doctor declared that the change was to him as an operation, for from the jolting he thought every one of his vertebræ would be dislocated. Probably the diminished state of my bag of rupees evidenced to the fact that the former bearers had been liberally paid, with which these would be well acquainted, and in compassion to my wife and the " wee bairn," and their own future comfort, suffered our ill manners to pass.

Fortunate indeed for us, for at that time

my Hindustani vocabulary was of the most
meagre character. I should have been quite
at a loss to find a village—to make myself
understood if I had; and I should have been
grieved to leave my wife and child alone in
so desolate a spot.

We had one pleasant break in the journey,
at Jubbulpore, which we were now approaching. It is a pretty little station, situated at
the base of a rocky hill, and about a mile
from the right bank of the Nerbudda river.
The hills are formed of granite, and the
bungalows are embowered in magnificent
clumps of bamboo.

We reached the dâk bungalow, and found
the station church opposite to it, and the
bell ringing for the week-day service.
After a bath, and whilst the dâk khit-
mutgar was searching in the bazaars for the
numerous delicacies he had promised us for
breakfast, I slipped away to church. The
chaplain seeing a stranger, introduced himself to me afterwards, came across and was
introduced to my belongings, and with Indian
hospitality insisted on our staying with him

I

and his wife, and resting for two or three days. The bearers, who always receive batta, or extra pay, for detention, offering no opposition, we gladly availed ourselves of the kindness.

Two months after, we were able to return it, for the station was besieged with the mutineers, and my friend, at his old trade again of soldiering, was mounting guard at the Residency. His wife and family he sent to me, and they remained with me until the country quieted down. He had been in the army, and present at the battle of Chillian-wallah.

In discussing that question, I remember his finishing up his description of the battle in the following, not very elegant, but graphic words, " Ah, it was an awful crush ! the fellows were upon us in myriads, shouting and yelling. As for me, I was so crowded that my elbows were above my ears, sword in hand. But alas ! the sword could make no impression on the fellows' turbans, so I took to sticking them ; and my dear sir, the sword went into their bodies, like a hot knife into a pat of butter."

We had now an opportunity of visiting the Industrial Institution here. The inmates were Thugs, who had all doubtless earned in their own estimation, by the murder of their fellow-creatures, their passport to heaven, but to whom individually the crime could not be brought home with sufficient force to fasten the hempen cord around their necks.

Colonel Meadows Taylor first became suspicious of this sect, in the year 1829. He discovered that parties of most respectable Mussulmans occasionally passed through his district, having charms, amulets, and medicines to sell. On questioning them, they replied, "that their trade was to take with them old and new sarees (women's cloths) and waistbands, getting in exchange brass and copper pots, and gold and silver ornaments; these we again exchange when the rains begin. We don't take our wives; they and the children remain at home as hostages for the rent we owe."

The colonel in commenting upon it says, "What could seem more plausible? and who could conceive the horrible crimes that were concealed under so fair a semblance?"

"The subject haunted me, why should so many men follow the same calling?

"Where did they go?

"Were they speaking the truth?

Two of his police, disguised as Fakirs, volunteered to follow and watch them; but he was recalled to his regiment, and it was left to Colonel Sleeman, in 1833, to discover and suppress the awful crimes of Thuggee.

Through the confession of one gang, the whole system was brought to light.

Their custom was to travel in gangs, and have in their company a good *improvisatore*, who entertained the wayfarers after their meal with their tales. Meantime, the accomplices each selected his victim and sat near him, and at a certain signal threw the rumāl, or throttling cord, round his neck, and rapidly finished the drama.

The bodies were then stripped and buried, or thrown into empty wells. Government invariably found the corpses of the victims where the approvers had notified them to be, either singly or in whole parties; but the details became so sickening as to preclude any further search than that absolutely necessary.

There were in the institution many of their children. All were now employed in weaving carpets, manufacturing tents—all of which from their excellence became famous in the market—and in making children's toys and covering them with an admirable coating of shell lac.

Mr. Ball, in his book, "Life in India," gives an account of how the lac is prepared, in the following words:—"Lac is secreted by an insect on the branches and twigs of certain jungle trees. It is collected by the forest tribes; where, however, there is a regular trade in shell-lac, propagation of the insect is systematically carrried on by those who wish for a crop. This is effected by tying small twigs, on which are crowded the eggs of the insect, to the branches of the khusum, i.e. *Schleichera trijuga, Butea frondens, and Zisyphus jujuba.*

"These insect eggs, or larvæ, are called 'seed.' They spread themselves over the branches, and secrete round them a hard crust of lac, which gradually spreads till it nearly completes the circle round the twig.

"At the proper season the twigs are broken off, and we must suppose them to have passed through several hands, and to have arrived at the manufactory.

"The lac is crushed off, washed, and stamped, from which a liquor comes, and is dried and placed in bags of cotton cloth.

"It is then subjected to the roasting of glowing charcoal, which melts the lac, which is formed into sheets of a rich golden lustre.

"A dark red liquor results from the washing, which is made into lac-dye, which, with the addition of mordants, yield the most brilliant scarlet dyes, not inferior, it is said, to the cochineal.

"The dye thus separated from the lac by washing is said to be the body of the insect."

We now found time to pay a visit to the "Marble Rocks," distant ten miles from the

THE MARBLE ROCKS.

Page 119.

cantonment, through the kindness of Colonel Sleeman, who lent us an elephant. They are situated in a most romantic position, traversed by the Nerbudda, that river where " the delicate waters sleep prisoned in marble," and whose waters, having furrowed for themselves a gorge of nearly two miles in extent, are " as clear as tears."

On either side rise up the huge masses of marble rock, veined here and there with dark green or black volcanic rock. They rear themselves some 120 feet in height.

Nothing can exceed the softly outlined colouring which white marble, toned down by the effects of climate, produces. The same effect I have noticed in the marble Taj at Aurungabad, of which might be said that which has been spoken of the Taj Mahal at Agra, of which it is a miniature copy, that it appears " as a beautiful thought softly bodied forth."

To add to the picturesqueness of the scene we saw a small hut in a cleft of the rock, wherein dwelt a real Fakir, the genius of the place.

> " Skirted with unhewn stone, it awes my soul,
>   As if the very genius of the place
>   Himself appear'd, and with terrific tread
>   Stalk'd through this drear domain."

He was a devout man, and painted, or rather striped, on his forehead and arms with many colours, intermingled with ashes. His garments were scanty, his frame emaciated, and his life said to be given to meditation,— a meditation at that time, I fear, not very favourable to the *Feringhee*, or European resident, in the country. He was seldom seen away from his hermitage, and was supplied by the natives with food.

> " He moved not, nor spoke, save in telling his beads
>   On the rosary strung of the jungle seeds."

My attendance at the church service introduced me to a captain in the Bengal army, whose first question was—

"Have you seen the last *Guardian?* If not, I will lend it you."

The regiment to which he was attached, soon after our introduction mutinied, went off to Delhi in a body, and left him alone in his glory.

He was then ordered to Nagpore, a civil station, and only ten miles distant from Kamptee, the military headquarters of the province. He had been forced into the army by his guardians, and now was determined to follow the profession upon which his heart was bent.

He took furlough, studied at Cambridge, and entered finally into Holy Orders. He had a very remarkable voice, and soon became elected a minor canon at one of our cathedrals. He was teaching himself music when we first knew him, and practised on a seraphine. He used at times to spend some days with us, and on one occasion having promised to do so, said he would bring his seraphine, as he preferred it to the piano for chants.

The day before he came he wrote in despair to say that the heat had so shrunk the wood of the instrument that he could not bring it. However, the next day he alighted from his bullock-carriage, seraphine and self, exclaiming,—

"All right, Padre. I have given it a bath,

and it goes better than ever; so let us have a chant."

The water had swelled the wood and restored the tone.

We now bade adieu to our kind entertainers, greatly refreshed with the rest, our minds busy with the interesting scenes through which we had passed, and our pittaras well supplied to meet commissariat difficulties.

CHAPTER VII.

Arrival at Kamptee—Climate—Cantonment—Cemetery —Extraordinary growth of trees—Method of transplanting—Sepulchral monuments—Small pox—Cholera camp—Different treatments of this disease— Jungle travelling—Making a carriage—Native cookery—Striking a light—Cheapness of travelling —Wild bullocks—Peculiar method of guiding—The "chamber in the wall"—Travelling with tents and herds—A fatal case of cholera in camp—The tamarind-tree and its effects.

"Experience is everything. It is seeing, and hearing, and trying; and arter that a feller must be a born fool if he don't know."

SAM SLICK.

WE have now reached Kamptee, the station which is to form our home for the next seven years to come.

It was a large military station, but at that time had been much denuded of troops on account of the Crimean war. There were not more than a couple of hundred European soldiers, artillerymen, in the station, a native cavalry regiment, and two native infantry ones, when we were startled by the outbreak of the Mutiny, so sadly famed in history.

This force was subsequently added to by a European infantry regiment, and the wing of a Lancer regiment.

The station was an extremely hot one, and yet less deleterious to the constitution of most people than the coast stations, with their combination of heat and damp. Here it was all dry heat, and in the height of the bad season there were scorching hot winds in the middle of the day, feeling like the blast from an open furnace, from which you recoiled as if smitten with fire. Punkahs of course went unceasingly day and night.

As sings George Sandys :—

"How often when the rising stars had spread
    Their golden flames, said I, 'Now shall my bed
    Refresh my weary limbs ; and peacefull sleepe
    My care and anguish in his Lethe steepe.'
    But lo ! . . . .
    When will the morning rise ?
    Why runs the chariot of the night so slow ?
    The day-star finds me tossing to and fro."

We rose early in the morning, about 4.30 or 5 a.m, our only chance of a breath of cool air. Were back a little after 7 a.m., when the house was shut up, the punkahs in full swing, and the thermantidotes also. Every available aperture from which the wind came was filled with a kus-kus (*Andropogon muriaticum*) tattie, or panel-work of this grass, over which water was thrown all day long. The hot wind passing through kept the thermometer generally below 90°.

I have known the temperature so high in the house as to necessitate putting water in your finger tumblers and glasses on the sideboard, otherwise they would go off every now and again with a pop.

Hot or the reverse, duty had to be performed, so in this station my bullock-coach was at the door about half-past ten, when the doctors had left, and the patients were comfortably breakfasted and settled down.

The chaplain visited hospital after hospital, holding service twice in the week; then came schools, orphanages, &c., until nearly time for luncheon—or tiffin, as it is called. The remainder of the day was at your own disposal, unless there should happen to be work to be done at the cemetery, or any church service.

The climate seemed to affect young children the most. Numbers were constantly the victims of teething; there was no railway within 200 miles, and the journey would in most cases be fatal, when the mandate was given to depart.

The cantonment ran north and south along the banks of a river. It possessed two large parade-grounds and an extensive drive termed the racecourse. There were good barracks for the European soldiery, and huts for the sepoys.

There was a large and commodious church, very unecclesiastical in appearance, and opposite to it a cemetery of about nine or ten acres. It was a dreary, uncared-for waste, with some fine old mimosa-trees, and a few pretty dark-leaved cork, with one central pathway.

All this was of course to be altered. So half a dozen gardeners, or *malis*, were engaged, and we commenced operations. We cleared out weeds, resodded graves, opened out paths, digging trenches alongside them wherein we planted roses and oleanders, Cape roses, myrtles, &c. Holes were dug for planting avenues of trees, and the trees themselves supplied from the young cork-trees scattered about, and by lopping off huge branches from the mimosa-trees. These, kept constantly watered, bore roots in a few weeks, and in less than three years it became necessary to—

> " Exert a vigorous sway,
> " And lop the too luxuriant boughs away."

I had a free supply of trees, flowering shrubs, &c., from the community, and ere many months had elapsed " God's acre " was a general resort. The soldiers and their wives frequently visited the cemetery, and one corporal, from the Emerald Isle, informed me once,—

" Ah, your riverence, shure an it will be a pleasure to be buried here."

I have never seen plants and shrubs so well removed as they are by the gardeners of the Central Provinces.

Suppose the shrub to be about five feet in height: four or five men will squat round it, *koorpee* in hand.

This is a short iron spud, a foot and a half in length, fastened into a handle.

They commence by picking away the ground at the distance of about a foot and a half from the stem of the plant or shrub, removing at intervals the loosened earth with their hands; and so they go on until they dig completely under the roots of the shrub, without disturbing the plant at all; they then bind it up with cords, haul it out, and replant it in a hole already prepared for its reception.

A few leaves will possibly fall away, but if previously uncared for, it is all the better for the removal and its plentiful supply of water. We sank a well, and so had abundance of water, which was led into the trenches at the pathway sides.

After this manner the natives irrigate their fields: the fields are divided into patches by ridges of earth; whilst then, one man sends forth the water from the well, another opens and shuts up these ridges as water is supplied.

The next step was to improve the character of the sepulchral monuments. For this purpose a dozen slabs of stone were procured from a neighbouring quarry. A mason was placed at each stone, on which I had traced in pencil the design. These were sold at cost price, and served as patterns for others.

In the neighbourhood was a species of fine sandstone, and also a fine hard kind of granite, which took an admirable polish.

The station was kept most scrupulously clean—and indeed this was a necessity, for we had frequent visitations of some disagreeable epidemic. Small-pox and cholera, the two most dreaded, seemed ready to break forth at any time.

One hot season we lost four hundred native children by the former disease. We dreaded the latter most.

During the time of the mutiny a detachment of soldiers was sent off to a neighbouring station, and on its return numbered, I

K

think, about one hundred and eighty—men, women, and children. Within two marches of the home station the water was bad, and cholera broke out.

Of course the detachment could not be allowed to enter the cantonment, and so were encamped on the opposite side of the river, the patients being accommodated in three large tents.

The number stricken were eighty—forty men, and the rest women and children. I shall never forget the melancholy scene as I entered the tents, one after another—to see the strong man, bowed down, livid as a corpse, the colour of lead, writhing in agony, and beseeching for water in piteous terms. Alas! in vain.

In those days it was deemed inexpedient to give them water, and they were supplied with peppermint water only, which seemed to add to their distress.

I buried forty of these poor people, who succumbed to the attack of this fell tyrant. For a terrible tyrant it is, inasmuch as the remedies efficacious in one season may be totally useless in another.

And this reminds me of an extraordinary visitation of a like character which broke out in Mysore.

A tramway was being constructed from Arconum on the Madras Railway to Conjeveram, where there were some very fine Hindoo temples, the object of many pilgrimages. The coolies employed were seized with cholera, and died in shoals, until by good fortune the acting engineer, Mr. Leahair, tried the experiment of an incision, introducing extract of Quassia.

This succeeded admirably, and rescued many from a state almost of collapse. This was narrated to me by Mr. Leahair himself, and it was confirmed to me in a peculiar manner.

I was called one day to see an engineer officer, who was not expected to live; he was suffering from disease of the liver.

He recovered, and told me that he had inspected the Conjeveram works, and had remarked a great number of natives with gashes in various parts of their bodies, and had inquired the cause.

Mr. Leahair informed him that they were his patients. The extract of Quassia had effected the desired cure, and the gashes were the healed incisions.

I have also heard of natives placing their cholera-stricken friends up to the neck in water. Possibly that might cure them, as in cholera, I have been told, it is want of water in the system which causes so much cramp.

At this station I had no water-highway to assist me in my out-station travelling. Ten miles from cantonment, and I found myself in the jungle.

I had to pass from village to village, until I reached by road and jungle my destination. Sometimes there was a church, sometimes none; but these periodical visits of the padre frequently led to the erection of one. The mess-house, or the assistant commissioner's, was put in requisition, and it was no uncommon order to hear the master say to his servant, "Butler, make church," which signified a large collection of chairs being brought together, and tables dispensed with.

Out-station duty generally commenced

after the cessation of the rains in October. Palkee-travelling and posting-horses were too expensive for constant journeys, and so for the most part chaplains had to resort to the two-wheeled gharrie, or bullock coach.

At times the travelling was easy enough, at others you had to go for miles over boulder-strewn plains. These boulders when broken up displayed a crystal interior, diversified with the most beautiful white, blue, and emerald-coloured facets. The boulders varied in size, say from a cricket to a football, and formed the most wearisome travelling. No springs could possibly stand such wear and tear for any continuance. The axles turned, and the tyres of the wheels snapped, or the wooden fellies of the wheel shrank. The village smiths were seldom skilful enough to repair these damages for any durable use, so there was nothing left but to build a cart after one's own devices.

My mode of construction was as follows. I had a strong framework of wood made, upon which boards were fastened to form the bottom of the cart; boards two feet in height made front and sides; there was also a small door at the back, with step.

Bamboos, secured by means of iron sockets, were bent over the body, upon which canvas, painted white, was stretched.

A stout bamboo with two lateral ones formed the pole, to which was attached a

BULLOCK CART.

wooden or bamboo yoke. A two-dozen beer case, inverted, formed the driver's and my servant's seat, upon which was placed some canvas, which, by the insertion of thin bamboos, acted as a tent when I bivouacked for the night, the bamboos being fastened to the centre pole of the cart.

Inside the gharrie was a front and back

seat, with a board to fill the intervening space and make a bed for me at night. A pair of country-cart wheels, procurable in any village bazaar, placed on a wooden axle the proper breadth of the country tracks, with two spare ones underneath in case of accident, completed the conveyance.

A brass basin, chair and table, were fitted inside the coach, together with leathern pockets to hold soda-water bottles.

In the well of the front seat I carried my provisions, such as tea, coffee, sugar, rice, &c. l started with daylight, and bivouacked near a village or by a stream of water at eventide. I could always procure eggs and chicken, and sometimes kid.

For refreshment during the day I found nothing so invigorating as cold tea ; the water was seldom to be trusted, and to qualify it with brandy was to make oneself very uncomfortable in the great heat of the day.

I had no springs to break, but after a little I became accustomed to the bumps and joltings, and could read with ease if not with tolerable comfort.

I travelled on an average between forty and fifty miles a day. Every five miles I changed my bullocks when able to do so. I dreaded, however, approaching a large village, as I knew delay would ensue in waiting for the fresh relay.

I carried a *purwannah*, or government order, enjoining the native officials to afford me every facility on my journey. I always took my native driver, and a table-servant who could cook for me, and very frequently thoroughly enjoyed my *al fresco* meals, which were prepared in no inartistic manner, for all East Indian natives are heaven-born cooks.

Your servant, when you stop for the night, sweeps a clear spot, selects three stones, on which he places an earthenware pot, scrapes out a little earth with his fingers, and kindles a brushwood fire, where the crackling of thorns may be heard, and his kitchen range is complete. But we must have a light, and this is how it is obtained, as described by Mr. Sanderson.

"A notch is cut in a stick as thick as one's little finger; this is laid on the ground and held down with the toes, the notched side being uppermost.

"The end of a stick about fifteen inches long, and as thick as an ordinary lead pencil, held vertically, is now inserted in the notch, the end being rudely sharpened.

"This is made to revolve rapidly between the hands under considerable downward pressure. The sticks soon commence to smoke at the point of contact, and a brown charred powder is worked out at the notch.

"In about a minute the friction kindles a spark in the powder, which is then taken up, placed in a piece of rag, with a handful of dry grass or leaves, and blown into a blaze."

The charge for the use of a pair of bullocks was one anna, i.e. three half-pence, per coss, a distance of two miles, and the man in charge of them usually had a small present.

The scene of the padre *en route* was one which would have entertained the loungers in Regent Street not a little; the coach going with a good pair of trotting bullocks at eight and ten miles per hour, and the owner, or man in charge of them, with his skirts tucked up, like Elijah of old, running for his life in front.

It was not always that you were fortunate enough to get good fresh bullocks, and the nature of the cultivation had a good deal to do with it. If *cholum* was abundant—a species of jawarree—the bullocks were in good condition, and you prospered; otherwise, you were ignominiously reduced to the pace of three miles an hour.

Sometimes the animals were wild and un-broken, and you found yourself brought up suddenly against a piece of rock or the stump of a tree. In such a case, snap went your axle, and there was no help for it but to turn everything out of your coach and put on an-other, and then move on again.

In the Hoshungabad district the animals were very untamed; they would submit to the yoke of the plough, but the coach was a strange object, to which they had an evident aversion.

The natives in that district had a strange way of guiding their cattle—not with the usual cord through the nostrils attached to the rein rope, but by a string fastened round the root of the horn.

To render this effective they beat the horn at its base, which made the part so sensitive that the least jerk served to guide the animal, whilst the horn itself shook with the paces of the bullock.

The natives at times are very cruel to their beasts. After hours of toil they still urge them to the uttermost, and when, exhausted, they lie down, they resort to the most cruel expedients, such as squeezing the juice of a chillie into the eye, to make them rise up again. Truly " the tender mercies of the wicked are cruel."

It is much the same with their treatment of horses. When once put into a gallop, they never cease flogging until the poor creature, covered with foam, falls exhausted, or comes to a standstill, unable any longer to proceed.

The station reached, after three days and nights of travel, the chief civilian has generally a " chamber in the wall " for the padre. There are the services to be arranged for, the schools examined, children baptized—of which there are generally a plentiful store—marriages solemnized, much pleasant intercourse, and no small hearty hospitality, and then the " ecclesiastic " proceeds to " pastures new," or returns to headquarters.

During my jungle travels in the Central Provinces, I frequently met a peculiar people, called Brinjaras.

They were the grain-carriers of India ere the railways were opened. They and their families travelled on foot with their flocks and their herds, the bullocks carrying the grain.

They were a fine-looking people, tall and lithe. The women were also tall, and had their arms covered with bracelets of ivory and other materials, and leglets too.

Mr. Ball writes of them: " I was informed by a Russian prince, who travelled in India in 1874, that one of his companions, a Hungarian nobleman, found himself able to converse with the Brinjaras of Central India in consequence of his knowledge of the Zingari language."

This probably accounts for their choice of a wandering profession, such as the gipsies have ever loved.

There was another mode of travelling more pleasant, but not so expeditious. Your departure was with tents, horses, palanquin, and perhaps an elephant or camel, lent to you by Government for their keep. The distance accomplished, ten miles a day, with a rest on Sunday. It was a very patriarchal procession, as you were accompanied by your servants, and they seemed anxious to take as many of their relatives with them as possible, and so your retinue became truly Abrahamic in its character.

There were men - servants and women-servants, horses and cows, sheep and goats, and in olden times you were allowed a *Naigue*, or corporal, with six Sepoy privates, to guard your luggage by day and your tents at night.

I had travelled over one hundred miles on this sort, on one occasion, and was about to enter my station on the following morning, when in the middle of the night the *Naigue* called me up to report that one of the privates was very sick.

The man was sleeping in the outer part of my tent, and I had heard occasional groans, but had not heeded them, as natives when not talking always seem to be grunting. In this case, however, I found the poor fellow suffering from all the symptoms of cholera.

We expected to reach cantonment the following day, but what was to be done in the meantime ?

At that period there was no inventive " Collis Browne." I had some opium and a few simple medicines. I bethought me of my camphorated chalk tooth-powder; so mixing some opium with that, I gave the patient a dose. It gave relief, and at daylight I sent him in to hospital. He succumbed, however, to the fatal disease the following day.

On this journey I was warned by the natives not to encamp under the inviting and umbrageous tamarind-tree (*Tamarindus Indica*) as likely to induce dysentery : the warning was a true one, and I avoided them ever afterwards.

CHAPTER VIII.

Privilege leave—A hill visit—Burning the grass—A
jungle on fire—Sitting up for a tiger—Fever, and
how to ward it off—A narrow escape—Mutiny
rumours—Outbreak at Nagpore—Intentions of
mutineers—Loss of children—Change of air—A
resurrection scene—Toilsome journey—Bombay—
Caves of Elephanta and Karli—Calicut—Beypore
—A happy mistake—Looking out for squalls—
Bangalore—Its first railway—A huge "Swami."

" Thou God of love ! beneath Thy sheltering wings
        We leave our holy dead
    To rest in hope !   From this world's sufferings
        Their souls have fled !

" Oh ! when our souls are burden'd with the weight
        Of life and all its woes,
    Let us remember them, and calmly wait
        For our life's close."

                        BOOK OF PRAISE.

THE rules of the service to which I am now
about to allude induced me to apply for three

months' "privilege leave," as I had been working for four years without any intermission of my duties. In the service, after every five months' duty the chaplains are allowed one month's rest; this is cumulative, and so you may get three months' leave after fifteen of service. No greater length of leave is granted than this; your place is supplied, and your full stipend paid to you.

A new sanatorium had been found out by Sir Richard Temple, in one of his world-wide scampers, at Mootoor, a doctor, engineer, and small company of sappers sent; so we determined to take our tents and household, and try and inhale some fresh air.

The place was invigorating after the plains, and did us good for a time. We had abundance of excitement at all events at night, for the *cheetahs* played around our tents, and were only kept off by the fires and natives on watch.

One day we were greatly disturbed to find the grass at the bottom of the hill on fire, the hillmen not having given us any warning of their intention to burn it.

JUNGLE ON FIRE.

I should here mention that the grass thus set fire to was that called spear-grass (*Andropogon aciculatus*), it grows in the central provinces to a height of two or three feet, and, as Mr. Sterndale says, must be felt to be appreciated.

It has, he says, a little sharp seed, bearing at one end a slightly-curved and barbed point, as acute as a needle, and at the other end a long awn like that of barley, and which has a similar property of working its way in by friction.

The flames were rapidly coming up with the wind. We turned out the sappers with branches of trees in hand, and made a clearing, which stopped the flames and saved the powder-magazine and disagreeable consequences.

Sanderson, in his interesting " Life among the Wild Beasts of India," gives an admirable description of a jungle on fire, which I have myself witnessed. It is true in all its details.

He says, " It is a magnificent sight to see the jungles of a hill-range burning. Some-

L

times immense tracts are on fire at once, and at night give forth a lurid blaze, which lights up the country for miles round.

" If the fire is near, the roaring noise is truly appalling, and impresses one with a sense of the dread power of the element.

" Huge pillars of thick smoke, in which lighted grass and leaves are whirled forward, roll heavily and slowly along, whilst a sound as of incessant discharges of small arms is caused by the bamboos and grass-stalks exploding.

" The noise lulls and swells with every alternation in the breeze, and in proportion to the thickness of the undergrowth.

" Long after the main conflagration has passed, isolated bamboo clumps and dried trees are seen burning fiercely like pillars of flame, till they fall over with a sullen crash and are quenched.

" Many trees smoulder for months. I knew one of enormous size, the roots of which, some of the girth of a bullock or greater, burnt for three and a half years, the fire smouldering slowly underground in the roots long after the parent stem had fallen."

Out of these charred embers of grass springs up a lovely verdant herbage, thoroughly appreciated by the lean cattle; and the natives are enabled thus to gather fruits not otherwise easily accessible.

I was invited one day by the doctor and engineer to accompany them in sitting up for a tiger, for whom we had set a trap in vain.

I was promised quarters in a tree, underneath which a goat was tethered. I expected to find a machān or platform prepared for me, whereon I could rest peaceably, rifle in hand, but nothing of the kind was ready, and I found myself eventually straddling across a couple of boughs, in far from a comfortable position.

This was at midnight. I endured this for some time with meek forbearance. I was not allowed to speak a word, indeed scarce to breathe, without being put down by these Nimrods with *Hush—ush—ush, he's coming !*

" But, my dear fellow," I whispered, " I am *tumbling* down. I've got the cramp."

I was shut up with " THERE, THERE *he is ;
look—creeping along that patch of grass.
Don't* be alarmed when he makes his rush."

" Don't you see him now ? "

I did not ; but I fancied I saw the long
grass quiver, and so I held on to the tree
and the heavy rifle.

" Ah ! " they said, after a pause, " he's
off ! *you* made a movement."

I don't believe I made any movement at
all; I only know I felt for a second as if my
heart was beating in my throat.

Daylight came; the sacrificial goat was
respited, and we went home, the air being
piercingly cold at this early hour.

It was pleasant to see the children sleeping peacefully, and my wife glad that no evil
had betided me.

I got fever for two days, the only occasion
on which I ever suffered from it in India,
with a residence of twenty years.

I have not the slightest doubt in my own
mind that much of the fever Europeans suffer
from in India is brought about either by
ignorance or carelessness. No one should

sleep, especially in the jungle, where there is constant miasma, without mosquito curtains.

The bed, or charpoy, should be well raised from the ground. And at night and in the early morning you should always keep within the influence of the camp-fires.

Should you feel any inclination to be feverish take a little quinine the first thing in the morning. There is no preventive equal to it, and you soon learn not to dislike its bitterness. Should that prove of none effect, then you must take arsenic under doctor's orders or go home, for it is seldom of any use going to the hills for this disease, and a fatal folly in the case of hepatitis.

The hill people hereabouts were very rough and uncouth, and only bearably civil when finding a good market for their goods. I do not think they would amass a large fortune on the profit of selling poultry, for I got a fine fat chicken for one anna, that is three halfpence, and smaller ones in proportion.

Solitude is very pleasant for a time, and

particularly so whilst your stock of literature is plentiful, but two months on the summit of a hill, with little in the way of exercise but that of descending the hill and ascending it afterwards, is apt to be tiring, and so we determined to return to headquarters.

Ere we do so I will narrate an incident, slight in itself, but which might have resulted in grave consequences to myself considering the temper of the natives towards Europeans at that time.

I was jogging along in the very heart of the jungle in my bullock coach with only my driver. The spot is vividly impressed on one of the cells of my memory; I see the very trees and shrubs in all their peculiarity of form, and the very formation of the sandy ground with its mixture of grass and bine under foot.

There was not an inhabitant for miles, as we had a long stage before us, when we suddenly came on a party of palkee-bearers returning to their villages. In all there were about fourteen men.

They stopped my coach very unceremoniously, and asked for roti (bread).

> "Like sturdy beggars, that intreat
> For charity at once, and threat."

Not liking the look of the men, and much less their manner, and fearing if I gave them anything they would *loot* (rob) me, I replied I was sorry I could not help them.

They let go my bullocks and went away, but only for a few hundred yards, when two of them returned, seized the bullocks' heads, and said they *must* have roti.

I had at that time no pistol or weapon of defence, but to hesitate was to be lost.

I jumped out of my coach, rushed at one of the men, whom I upset; the other, with a *ya! ya!* fled.

I took advantage of my success, jumped into the gharrie again. My driver, thoroughly frightened, agreed with me in thinking "prudence the better part of valour," seized the bullocks' tails, gave them a twist and a thwack, and off we went as hard as we could go. Fortunately they did not attempt to follow us, and so we escaped a further rencontre.

I have referred to the Mutiny *en passant,* but we were only just touched by it. We had our frights, scares, and anxieties; we read of the atrocities committed, and the brave and heroic manner in which they had been endured.

Expecting to hear momentarily that our next-door neighbour, Secunderabad, one of the most important stations in the Presidency, had succumbed to the general disaffection, we were only slightly troubled to hear of smaller stations having revolted. At Nagpoor there was a Ressalah regiment of Bengalees, and we feared them, though their officers believed in them with a lunacy only curable by the bullet, and our fears were realized.

They mutinied, were on the point of mounting their horses, when the plot was revealed to their European commandant, just in time to save both cantonments.

They had kindly devised the old idea of firing the thatch-roofed bungalows, shooting down the officers and disposing of the ladies, and knocking out the brains of the little ones.

They were disarmed under the presence of our small force of artillery, and seventeen of the ringleaders hanged. A more villainous-looking crew I never saw in irons before.

This state of living in constant expectation of something disagreeable turning up was extremely unpleasant, in addition to the discomfort of being turned out of your bungalow to take up your quarters for the night under the protection of guns and gunners, with port-fires ready lighted.

Meantime, numberless fugitives came in from surrounding stations in evil plight and scant clothing.

Our good bishop had died, and another Pharaoh had ascended the episcopal throne. He listened to my tale of heat and exile, and I was ordered to Bangalore, the garden of Southern India.

I had experienced my share of hard work and deep sorrow. In the seven years I had lost two of my children, and been compelled to bury the latter myself. They now rest in peace in the beautiful cemetery we had so unknowingly prepared for their reception.

> " O what is man, to whom thou should'st impart
> So great an honour as to search his heart;
> To watch his steps, observe him with thine eye,
> And daily with renew'd afflictions try ? "

Southey has caught with intuition the key-note of the Church's burial service, when he writes,—

> " Nature hath assign'd
> Two sovereign remedies for human grief:
> Religion, surest, firmest, first and best,
> And strenuous action next.

" Therefore be ye steadfast, immovable, always abounding in the work of the Lord, forasmuch as ye know that your labour is not in vain in the Lord."

In the latter case referred to, a sweet little girl of ten months had not strength to cut her teeth. Who can describe her winning ways and wistful glances as she lies in our arms, wearily walking hour after hour, coaxing her to sleep? The order at last comes —the child must be taken away, her only chance, to a cooler place.

The only place a degree or two cooler was

the small out-station of Seonee, belonging to another presidency, and that sixty miles distant. This station only has a few bungalows and a rude pile of buildings occupied by the Assistant Commissioner, which had formerly been the palace of Mahomed Amin Khan, the Mohammedan ruler of the place. Since that time a handsome church and other buildings have been erected.

The heat and motion of the journey only produced delirium, and then the "little one" found refuge in the bosom of the Saviour of whom she had never heard.

The cemetery was so uncared for that we determined to take her into Kamptee, that the two might sleep side by side. A messenger was sent to have all in readiness at any hour. It was a journey burnt into my memory, never to be effaced. The heat and glare of the arid waste over which we travelled, the solitariness with which I companied alone, in one desolate spot under a leaf-thatched shed with my precious burden whilst the bearers were resting for a short space, will ever haunt me.

A night and a day I travelled, reaching my home at midnight; and then, hastening "to bury my dead out of my sight" by torchlight, with only two or three to witness my weakness, I buried and wept.

Ah! what a glorious resurrection scene of innocent children will one day take place in that saintly-thronged spot! What a rustle of angel-wings will there be bearing the re-collected bodies to the gates of heaven!

> "Oh! let no tear thine eyelids dim,
>   O'er this pale form of clay;
> But think she rests at peace with Him
>   Who wipes all tears away!"

We were now appointed to Bangalore. It was a long and toilsome journey to undergo, as preparations had to be made for so many different forms of travelling—from palkee to rail, rail to steamer, then rail, and finally horse dâk.

After two hundred miles of palkee travelling we had the pleasing sight of parallel iron rails, and after a few miles of *trolly* travelling, came to the great "iron horse" and comfortable carriages.

All railway carriages in India are double-roofed, the outer overlapping the inner roof. The windows also have additional venetians. When we first arrived at Bangalore the railway to that station was not completed.

I remember well its opening, and the astonishment it caused amongst the native population. I can vouch for the truth of the following conversation, which was narrated to me by the chief engineer of the railway, who told me he heard it himself :—

SCENE : *the engine approaching.*

RAMMOSAMMY : " What a huge swami ! " (that is deity).

" Yes," replies MOOTOOSAMMY, " but how did they get Shitan into him ? "

The latter native, it will be seen, was under the impression that the Evil Spirit was bound inside the engine and caused it to move, but in what manner captured and confined, he could not comprehend.

RAMMOSAMMY then answers, " *Oh, by the Governor-General's hookum,*" that is command.

To go on with our journey. We arrived

safely at Bombay, where we remained a few days, waiting for a steamer to take us to Calicut. I took the opportunity whilst here of visiting the cavern and rock temples of Karli and Elephanta, with which travellers are now so familiar. The architecture of the caves is monumental in character, possessing much of the colossal grandeur and vastness of the Egyptian style, with which it harmonizes in general outline and design.

Its effect, however, as the Rev. P. Perceval remarks, is different :—" Substitute for Isis, the tri-faced figure of the Hindoo triad and its various symbols, and in the place of lightness and calm repose, stillness and an air of tranquillity, you have gloom and horror-inspiring representations.

To reach Karli you have to ascend the Western Ghats, and in a village of this name is the famous cave.

It is a fine, if not one of the finest of the Buddhist monuments. The doorways and *façades*, its rows of columns with elephants carved in stone for capitals, its arched and ribbed roof, and, most peculiar of all, its cells in the face of the rock, and spring of pure water issuing from its base, will always leave its impress on the memory of the visitor.

We had been anxious about the health of one of our children, who was suffering from dysentery, and which the heat, fatigue, and bad food of the journey had not improved. A few hours, however, at sea put the child all right, and he was quite convalescent at the end of a week.

There is nothing so supremely good for this complaint as sea air; that, with careful dieting, will conquer very frequently the most stubborn cases.

On board we were shown to our cabin, and had got all things *en règle;* then having taken a turn on deck for fresh air, we descended to dress for dinner.

Imagine our dismay at finding all our goods and chattels turned out upon the cuddy floor *sans cérémonie.*

It appeared that the cabin had been bespoken by a newly-married couple some time beforehand, and so there was nothing for it but to submit. My wife and children got located in the ladies' cabin, and I slept very contentedly on deck.

The gentleman who had so unceremoniously treated us, was a "coffee planter," and said to have amassed a good deal of money. He certainly had expended a good deal in flash jewellery. Little incidents are amusing on a voyage, and this couple served to amuse the passengers, who were frequently finding them examining their rings with childish interest.

We had a very pleasant voyage down the coast, touched at different ports, where the scenery was beautiful to the eyes of jungle travellers, and especially the Portuguese settlement of Goa.

We arrived at Calicut, a most uninviting-looking place, hot, dry, and sandy, with a miserable collection of daub-and-wattle huts on the beach.

On the voyage our friend the "coffee planter" had attracted no little attention by his anxiety to obtain the choicest viands for his own peculiar delectation; and directly we stopped he was first off and away, as afterwards appeared, to engage a conveyance for himself and wife to Beypoor.

This was distant eight miles, and it was here we were to join the railway. In due course of time we procured a boat or canoe, a wretchedly-frail-looking structure, in which we safely got to shore. No sooner had we landed than we found an excellent carriage, in which I placed my wife and children, thankful, as we thought, for the happy chance. Telling our dusky coachman to go to Beypoor, we started.

It was a most charming drive through the most picturesque country, teeming with vegetation. There was the huge "Jack" tree (*artocarpus*) with its queer, cumbrous-looking fruit, at least two feet in length and one in breadth, *on branches and roots*, and its dark, shining leaves. There was the tall and equally curious-looking "Palmyra" tree, some seventy feet in height, with all its fan-like leaves on its top; the broad-leaved plantain with its cool, refreshing, and broad-spreading leaves—each sufficiently large to

M .

serve as a blanket—and strange spikes of golden fruit; the graceful cocoa-nut, and tall and slender betel-nut-tree too, shooting up towards heaven; and as a groundwork to all this, against the red, dusty road, were

> " Places enfolding
> Sunny spots of green,"

the emerald green paddy (or rice) fields, dotted over prettily enough with the small, white paddy bird, a kind of stork.

We reached the Dâk Bungalow. It contained a good-sized sitting and bedroom, and partitioned off, were two much smaller rooms, fit only for creeping things. It was the dreariest and dirtiest of Dâk bungalows, and mine was no mean experience; and to crown all, was situated on the banks of a narrow, dirty canal.

On paying the driver of the carriage, he presented to my notice for the first time a scrap of paper whereon was written the name of the " Coffee Planter ! " It was too late to remedy the mistake at the end of the comedy, and so we entered and ordered dinner.

The dinner was a particularly good one, and though not cooked in a very *récherché* manner, much better than we could have anticipated. We did ample justice to it, and thought our lot cast in more favourable lines than we could have hoped for.

We retired to rest, but our slumbers some two or three hours afterwards were disturbed by a great hubbub. The " Coffee Planter " had arrived ; we had not only appropriated his *gharrie*, but evidently his *dinner*. Thus was I innocently avenged of mine enemy without any *malice prepense.*

How wonderfully does the goddess of Fortune balance inequalities !

On the following morning *we met*, but he avoided my glance, and we did not travel in the same compartment.

After a bullock-coach the iron horse is a decided luxury, and we were speedily set down at Tripatore. Here we had to leave the royalty of locomotion, and proceed the last eighty miles by bullock or horse transit.

Cholera was reported on the road, and so we chose the more expensive but expeditious

way. We slept at a nice, clean Dâk bungalow for one night, and accomplished the
whole distance in two days.

But who can describe the bumps and the
thumps of such a journey at full speed, over
roads unmended after the rainy season ?

The horse transit was a huge machine on
four wheels, with a framework covered with
a mattress, whereon we sat tailor-fashion.
My place was at the window near the driver,
keeping a good look out for the ruts, and
giving warning of impending danger to my
family as occasion required.

On starting we frequently had to expend
half an hour in coaxing the horses to make a
start; poor things, experience had taught
them that when once forced into the gallop
they would be unmercifully belaboured, until
exhausted nature brought them to a standstill, or we arrived at the place for change
of quadrupeds. There is an end to all journeys, and this happily found us in the
presence of the smiling landlord of the
Cubbon Hotel.

CHAPTER IX.

Bangalore—Its aspect—The Pettah—Fruits and flowers
—The legend of the moon-creeper—Establishment
of Bishop Cotton's School and College—Female
branch—Its success—The Eurasian drummers—
—Ragged schools—History of St. Paul's Mission
Church—Church Restoration—Branch Mission—
Expedient for making ground glass—New use of
blue granite—Curious method of quarrying.

"Blessed be God, for flowers!
For the bright, gentle, holy thoughts that breathe
From out their odorous beauty,
        Like a wreath of sunshine on life's hours."

AFTER Secunderabad in the Deccan, Bangalore is probably the largest military station
we possess in South India. It is most un-
tropical in its aspect, possessing very few
Palmyra, date or cocoa-nut trees ; and yet an
abundance of other beautiful flowering ones,
such as the tulip and "*Poinceana regia*," or
" Gold Mohur Tree."

The cantonment runs east and west in a long stretch. There are three very large parade-grounds; a military force of European cavalry, horse and foot artillery, and infantry; native regiments of infantry, and some companies of sappers and miners.

There are three chaplains who each have a church, and there is a small Church of England Mission chapel. There are Roman Catholic churches and priests, a Presbyterian church and minister, Wesleyan chapel and *missionaries so called.*

A fort and arsenal, with a palace once belonging to Hyder Ali also. There are good bungalows, hotels, shops, market-place, and railway-station. Fine public buildings for the different Government offices, large Government schools for native education, reading and assembly rooms, a band-stand and public gardens.

On the whole it is a grand station, and considered the most healthy in the Madras Presidency. There is the Pettah or native city, with its flat-roofed houses looking hundreds of years old, and monkeys innumerable scrambling over them. The climate is favourable alike for fruit and flowers : thus we have apples, strawberries, peaches, native fruits, such as guava, custard-apple, pummelo, mango, amongst the former ; roses and caladiums, begonias, fuchsias, ferns, violets, Borgonvillea, and other creepers, and passion-flowers amongst the latter.

One of the most beautiful creepers is called the moon creeper. Its flower comes out at sunset, and bears an enormous convolvulus-shaped flower of pure white. The natives in the south of India, writes Mr. Robinson, have a legend, the

"Legend of the Moon Flower."

There was once, they say, a maiden, exceedingly beautiful, and modest as she was beautiful.

To her the admiration of men was a sorrow from morning to night, and her life was made weary with the importunities of her lovers. From her parents she could get no help, for they only said, " Choose one of them for your husband, and you will be left alone by the others."

From her friends she got less, for the men called her heartless, and the women said her coyness would be abandoned before a suitor wealthier than her village wooers.

But how could they know that one evening soft and cool, as the maiden sat at her father's porch, and there were no eyes near but the little owls' on the roof and the fire-flies under the tamarinds, there had come out from the guava-trees a strange youth, who had wooed her and won her; and who with a kiss on her fair, upturned face, had sealed the covenant of their lovo?

But she knew it; and sitting when the evenings were soft and cool, at her father's porch, she waited for the stranger's return.

But he never came back; and her life, sorely vexed by her lovers, became a burden to her, and she prayed for help to the gods.

And they in their pity for her, turned her into a great, white moon-plant, which clinging to her father's porch, still waits in the evening, with upturned face for the truant's kiss !

For commissariat purposes the fine Hurry-arah grass makes excellent hay, and with the grafted mangoes in your compound helps much in paying the rent.

I had a fine bungalow, called " Sidney Park," which cost 12*l.* per month rent, un-furnished, and I realized 20*l.* with all ex-penses of cutting defrayed on the grass, and 12*l.* on the mangoes.

In thinking over the needs of the district now given to me in charge, the most urgent want appeared to me to be that of a good middle-class school. I was the more inclined to take this in hand as it was one of the most urgent wants of the time, and as several parents had requested me very urgently to do so.

I had assisted in establishing such an institution in Nagpoor, and one somewhat similar in character was required here. For want of some such institution numbers of my people, such for instance as the children of clerks, were being educated by the Roman Catholics; not that they were in any degree hostile to the Church of England, but that they required Church schools at a moderate cost.

There was an excellent college on the Neilgherries, but the means at the disposal of the class requiring assistance did not enable many to avail themselves of the education there offered.

Supposing one son to be educated, the cost prevented the education of the remaining children. The want was really a crying one, for, on the one hand, we had grand Governmental schools imparting a first-rate education to *pure natives*, whilst *the mixed race* were being utterly neglected. It is true there were some institutions at the Presidency, but the same objections of distance and expense held good of them.

As regards Bangalore, the education out of it involved boarding-out expenses, and either a severer climate or an inferior one.

My plan, therefore, was to form a college and school primarily for the East Indians, good enough to include the children of

European officers if need be, where education might be obtained on Church of England principles, at a moderate cost and in a good climate.

I foresaw that should such a scheme be practicable, incalculable good would result, and that we should be permeating the most important class in the community.

I selected Bishop Cotton's scheme of education for the hills, adapting it to the plains. The scheme, not to weary the reader, was forwarded to the Supreme Government, obtained the assistance of the good bishop, of Sir Richard Temple, and Sir Charles Trevelyan.

All other schemes had eliminated the female element, that objection, through the greatest opposition and amid innumerable difficulties, I succeeded in overcoming. And I am well rewarded by the appearance of the following extract from an Indian paper.

It is headed "THE MARCH OF FEMALE EDUCATION." "From the list of the candidates who have passed the matriculation examination held in December last, we notice that six young ladies have been successful, all educated in Bishop Cotton's College, Bangalore. The Rev. Dr. Pope is to be congratulated on the success that has attended his efforts. Bishop Cotton's College is the only institution which has passed out female matriculates and first in Arts in the Madras Presidency."

The scheme took quite twelve months ere all the primary difficulties were overcome, and the institution set on foot. It was named after the originator of the Hill scheme, and varied indeed for the first two or three years were its fortunes.

It cost me many a sleepless night and anxious day. There was a powerful Presbyterian and Roman Catholic influence against the lines upon which the scheme was based, and at one time it would have come to an untimely end had it not been for the talents and self-denying labour of General Hill, R.E., and Captain Lavie, who nobly came to my assistance. I could have commanded any amount of pecuniary help had I been induced to place the college and school on an undenominational basis. But I felt that the Church of England was strong enough to hold her own, and I did not desire a more liberal basis than she could give.

I was able finally to obtain the services of the Rev. Dr. Pope, than whom none could have been more fitted for the wardenship.

Large and handsome buildings have been erected for both institutions, which, though separated by the warden's house, adjoin.

No need of much reflection to see the needs of my new district. It is varied enough in its character and in its wants.

Take a walk along the lines of the native infantry regiments, and see in abundance the children of the Christian drummers. These people were all Eurasian, that is a mixture of Europe and Asia. They were too poor to be admissible in their rags to the schools already in existence, so a ragged school was started for them.

I had a small building given me, I employed a dame to teach, and prepared them for the duties of the day by beginning with a meal.

This robbed the bazaars of many an importunate little mendicant, and I hope did no little good; anyhow, it formed the nucleus of doing much, as this history will show in another place.

I have alluded to a Church of England mission chapel. This was in my district, the secretaryship being held temporarily by another chaplain until my arrival.

Nothing well could be more plain or ugly than the building used as the mission chapel. It was an oblong structure, with plastered walls, holes for windows, and wooden shutters for the holes.

In the interior was a brick and mortar construction, nine feet in height, to serve as pulpit. A common table for an altar, covered with an old red baize cloth. Seats there were none, as there seldom are in native churches, mats serving the purpose more appropriately.

A verandah running on the north and south sides of the church kept out the sun. The compound or church enclosure was surrounded with a low mud wall, and at the entrance-gate there was a triangle such as it was customary to punish recalcitrant drummers upon, from which was suspended a cracked bell to summon the worshippers.

Miss Gordon-Cumming, in her interesting book "At Home in Fiji," tells us that the native Christians were summoned to public worship by the beating of a wooden drum or *lali*.

This lady writes : "On Sunday we walked along the shore, and then by a path through the abandoned sugar-fields till we came to a little native church, where, much to our amusement, the teacher told us that he regulates the hour of service by the opening of a *brauhinia* blossom. He has no clock, but when the flower opens he beats the wooden *lali* or drum, and then the people assemble.

"We watched this floral time-piece expand its blossoms to the early light, and then the congregation came."

To return to the mission.

There was a native deacon in charge, who resided in a portion of the native schools, opposite to the church, a neat and appropriate building. His stipend came from the " Venerable Society for the Propagation of the Gospel in Foreign Parts," and the schools were maintained by voluntary contributions.

In a large station the chaplains have little leisure for any but their own immediate work. At the cemetery morning and evening, church services, endless committee meetings, schools and hospitals requiring daily attention, only a passing interest was likely to be taken in the mission. Yet from the records it appears that the mission owed what little life it had to them; they had probably " done what they could." For most chaplains feel what Bishop Milman has expressed, that to a certain degree " they are as responsible before Christ for the heathen as for the British soldier, and that there is no evading the responsibility by any one who undertakes an Indian chaplaincy."

Missionary work has a peculiar fascination of its own. This feeling is greatly stirred up within one in India, one of its grandest arenas—indeed, the largest field yet seen in the world for Christian enterprise.

Surrounded with natives, who supply your every want, many of them abounding with simplicity, and possessing the most Christian feelings without being aware that they are such, must touch the heart of any European, much more that of a Christian pastor, who by his ordination vows is bound " to seek for Christ's sheep that are dispersed abroad, and for His children in the midst of this naughty world, that they may be saved through Christ for ever."

Some of the most faithful, affectionate, and unselfish of servants are to be found midst the "poor heathen," and "perishing savages" of the East. Dismissing such terms for " the good of all nations," let us fear lest we of Christian countries should be found poorer, as Bishop Selwyn remarks, who have received so much and can account for so little.

To create a new interest in the mission and obtain funds to make its church a more fitting place for divine service, I searched its meagre records, and give the result to my reader. I wrote : " The mission was first planted during the last century by some German missionaries

N

in connexion with the Society for Promoting
Christian Knowledge.

"It was then transferred to the 'Society
for the Propagation of the Gospel,' and
managed by a committee at Madras.

"The first renewed spark of life, however,
given to it, seems to have been in 1817, when
a chaplain again gathered together the
scattered congregation. For nineteen years
more the little mission appears to have
struggled on with varying success under the
greatest disadvantages. Their only place of
worship was a small schoolroom, and the
sacraments were administered by the chaplain at St. Mark's Church, in a language not
understood of the people.

"Under the charge of another chaplain,
now Canon Trevor of York, the mission was
reconstituted, additional schools opened, and
a church built, partly by subscription, and
partly by the 'Society for Promoting Christian Knowledge,' called by Daniel Wilson,
'The Primitive Missionary Society of
India.'

"This church was consecrated on the 31st

of March, 1840, under the title of 'St. Paul's Mission Church,' for native Christian worship only. Daily prayer was established, with full Sunday services, and stated administration of the sacraments in the native tongue.

" Finally, a missionary was appointed by the 'Society for the Propagation of the Gospel,' and a mission house erected by local subscription. In 1851 the late Bishop Dealtry licensed a native priest to the charge ; but he was soon withdrawn, owing, it is believed, to his being wanted for a more important charge, and thus the prospects of this mission became again overclouded.

" Since the year 1845 there have been five elementary schools and one central one ; but the former were abandoned on the withdrawal of missionary in charge, although there were as many as 205 children receiving Christian instruction in them."

" From 1845 (the earliest date of registering) to the present time, there have been fifty-nine adult converts from heathenism to Christianity, and 216 infants admitted into Christ's fold by the sacrament of baptism.

" At the present time (1864) the Mission has only one native deacon, one catechist, a schoolmaster, and a mistress. The number of the native congregation is about 300. The communicants average sixty, and all these have been previously instructed. There are two schools attached to the mission : a boys' school, containing between forty and fifty children, and a girls' school, with about thirty girls. The latter are provided with a meal daily, and are clothed once a year.

" For the last two years, through paucity of funds, the children have been clothed at the expense of a benevolent lady in the station. During the past year, also, twenty-five of the poorest Christians have been clothed by subscription. With the present small missionary staff, any aggressive measures such as now contemplated against heathendom, would be impossible. For what are these among so many ? It is only sufficiently large to carry on cantonment work on a small scale—a reproach which it is hoped will now be speedily removed.

"The following statement will show the result of last year's work, and, we trust, stir the hearts of many to help liberally the proposed new movement. Under the active working of the Rev. J. Eleazer, the native deacon, who was ordained by Bishop Gell in 1861, there have been thirteen adult heathens brought to Christianity. The selection of names on admittance to Christianity may interest those to whom I appeal, and therefore I append them :—

Heathen Name.	Christian Name.
Mootoo	Isaac
Manjathal	Rebecca
Monian	Jacob
Monian	Joseph
Pappathy	Mary Catherine.
Palagamaly	Thomas
Mootoo	Ephraim
Thanjalan	Manasseh
Theonnah	Priscilla
Kempy	Magdalene
Annamal	Christiana
Pappal	Ruth
Augamal	Catherine.

"One Roman Catholic has been admitted into the church; seventeen children have been baptized; all the offices of religion diligently attended to, and the Blessed Sacrament administered by the chaplains of the station. The congregation has so far increased as to necessitate enlargement of the sacred fabric, and many alterations, which are now in progress."

It will be seen from this account that restoration had commenced. 100*l.* had been collected, and the appeal produced about 200*l.* more. The mission was intended only to grapple with the Tamil population, but it was now proposed to extend its usefulness to the Canarese, of whom there were *five millions.* It was also designed to open mission-rooms for service in some of the neighbouring villages. This was done at Oossoor, where there was a good opening from the number of horse-keepers employed at the Government remount depôt.

From this time, in two years we had an encouraging mission, with a native deacon, the Rev. A. Sebastian.

This clergyman has now worked with marked success for many years in Secunderabad.

The mother church · was not sufficiently large now for the worshippers, and so we determined to add a chancel; before, it had none. In this we placed a very handsome east window. We could not afford stone for the mullions, and so we made them of good sound teakwood. It was glazed with white ground glass, with a ruby cross in the centre. The constant and intense glare of the sun renders any colouring pleasing, and a relief to the eye. But good coloured glass was immensely expensive, though we had a sufficiency of it presented to us.

I and one of my schoolmasters accomplished the glazing, at which we became great adepts. To find a sufficiency of white ground glass was our next difficulty, for that also was very expensive; so I adopted the following plan, which succeeded admirably.

I placed a woman coolie on the ground with an even board before her, some very fine river sand, and two diamond-shaped quarries of glass, and an earthen vessel of water, and told her to rub the two surfaces together with the sand between them. After five minutes' labour, the plain glass was converted into ground glass. The woman's wages were threepence per diem. The common glass I bought very cheaply in the bazaar; and so that difficulty was conquered.

We put in new windows, each protected with outside venetians, glazed them with white ground glass, and added a coloured border.

At the west end of the church we built a very deep porch, surmounted by a pretty bell turret.

A vestry at the east end, replastered walls throughout, and the nave roof spandrilled, completed the whole.

A new and handsome altar properly vested, a super altar, with white alabaster cross and other fittings, completed the chancel. Of course, reading-desk and pulpit were introduced; font from England and alms-box completing the nave.

Nothing could exceed the delight of the native people. They felt that the faith held by the Europeans' chaplains (for I was helped much by the Rev. J. Bull and the Rev. Gilbert Cooper) and their countrymen, was *one*, and identical with their own.

How true the lines of the saintly Keble—

" He too is blest, whose outward eye
  The graceful lines of art may trace
While his free spirit, soaring high,
  Discerns the glorious from the base :
Till out of dust his magic raise
A house for prayer, and love, and full harmonious
  praise."

Once in the month I had to administer the Blessed Sacrament to the native congregation, and this I learnt to do after a time in Tamil. When all this had been accomplished, the compound wall was next taken in hand.

There is a substratum of bluish granite running a few feet under the surface of the earth in many parts of Bangalore. This was quarried in flakes, their thickness being determined by the mode of quarrying.

The method was this. The length and breadth of the stone required was first marked out in charcoal. Then fire was placed at certain intervals along this line, holes drilled here and there, and according to the time the fire was allowed to burn, was the thickness of stone obtained, and this was ascertained by occasional tappings with sledge-hammers on the surface. This stone I found constantly used for the foundation of houses, and occasionally for pillars.

The thought struck me that if I obtained it in sufficiently thick blocks, and dressed the edges, it would make a very seemly wall, and so it did.

Government took a lesson from my example, and afterwards built an entrance to the cantonment cemetery with stone dressed in the manner described, that is, rough inner surface and dressed edges.

CHAPTER X.

Purchasing children—Establishing orphanage—European pensioners—Pensioners' church, and how it
was built—Consecration—Incumbent—Journey to
Ootacamund—Tonjons—Muncheels—Ghaut scenery
—Coonoor —Climate of the hills—Sholas—Vegetation—Hill ornithology—Todas and their habitations—Ancient tithes—Church pioneering.

" Come, and I will show you what is beautiful."

In founding a ragged school I had always
regarded it, more or less, only as a temporary
measure of relief for the indigent and neglected waifs and strays of society.

Another chaplain might come and evince
no interest in the work, funds might fail,
and the whole thing collapse. So I impressed on my mind that an orphanage was
in some way or another to spring from this,
when all at once the opportunity was given
me for taking up the work.

It came about in this wise. I was sitting in the heat of the day in my verandah, thinking chiefly of how to get cool, when an old native woman, with dark face—looking all the darker from her grey hair—presented herself, with two pretty little flaxen-haired girls, asking an alms.

I immediately asked her where she got the children, who were evidently of European extraction.

She replied that they were her daughter's children, that her daughter was dead, and their father had gone to Europe with his regiment.

Here was a legacy the noble British soldier had left behind him !

In a large garrison station what was to be the future of these poor little waifs ? It was too frightful to contemplate. Surely there ought to be some refuge for the helpless destitute !

I said to her, " Now look here, granny. I will buy those little ones of you (utterly regardless of the laws relating to slave-dealing); I will feed, clothe, and educate them, and try

and make them good women. You shall
come and see them as often as you like, but
they are to be my children. I will give you
thirty rupees for them (3*l.*)."

The bargain was struck.

She assented, remarking very sensibly
that she had not long to live, that it was with
difficulty she could procure food for them,
and that she should die happily if she thought
the Padre-Sahib would take care of them,
and as he had made the promise, she knew
he would.

I lost no time in hiring a small house near
one of my schools, engaging a matron, purchasing a few mats for beds, and some
crockery, adding to the establishment two
orphan children out of my ragged school, in
less than a week two more destitute children
turned up, and so the " Orphanage and Refuge for Destitute Children" became an
accomplished fact, in Bangalore.

" Moments there are in life, alas, how few !
    When, casting cold prudential doubts aside,
    We take a generous impulse for our guide,
    And following promptly what the heart thinks best,
    Commit to Providence the rest ;

Sure that no after-reckoning will arise
Of shame or sorrow, for the heart is wise.

And happy they who thus in faith obey
Their better nature ; err sometimes they may,
And some sad thoughts lie heavy in the breast,
Such as by hope deceived are left behind ;
But like a shadow these will pass away
From the pure sunshine of the peaceful mind."

In pushing the fortunes of an Orphanage fewer difficulties presented themselves than in establishing other institutions.   Every one would give a little to an acknowledged want of the kind, of whatever denomination, and so the establishment, though based on Church of England principles, received help and sympathy from all.

I was nobly supported by my parishioners in the establishment of this Institution, and more especially by Sir Frederick Haines, the General of the Division, by the Rev. Dr. Murphy, and also by the generous and active assistance of Colonel and Mrs. Rammell, of of the Madras Army.

After a time Government gave 72*l.* a year for educational expenses ; and in the course of five years a handsome building was erected, sufficiently large to accommodate 100 children, at a cost of 50,000 rupees, otherwise 5000*l*.

It has now been in existence for nearly sixteen years. Numbers have been admitted, taught useful trades, and sent forth to battle with the world.

Before leaving Bangalore I had the pleasure of baptizing the first child of one of my first orphans, having married her to a respectable tradesman twelve months previously.

One portion of the district assigned me comprised a small colony of European pensioners. This community had served their time in the army or other employment, and been pensioned.

For the most part they had married East Indian or Eurasian women, and some even natives, and had thus exiled themselves for the remainder of their lives from their native land.

No more would they see " Sweet Auburn, lovely village of the plain." The experiment had been tried of transplanting their East

Indian wives; but the cold climate never suited their constitutions, and they sickened and died off.

They were, moreover, totally unfitted for a European life and its labours. Many of these people had large families of copper-coloured children. What could they possibly do with them?

It was sad enough to see them in such a plight, and more still to perceive the deterioration in their habits and feelings which such intermarriage had produced.

My church was already crowded with troops and officers, and there was little room for these poor people.

Hence the necessity of erecting a church for them, that they might enjoy the means of grace.

Such a scheme had been devised four or five years previously, but had come to nothing. A few hundred rupees had been collected and placed in a bank, but all interest seemed to have died out.

A small site at the corner of a parade-ground seldom used, had been given; this, under two successive generals of division, I had got enlarged to such an extent as to admit of building the Orphanage on one side with abundant space for the church in the centre.

I drew a plan for the church, which, I am happy to say, was rejected by the Church Building Society of Madras as too small, and was succeeded by one designed by the accomplished Government architect, Mr. Chisholm, fully adapted for the purpose.

My time, however, was drawing nigh for my hill tour of duty. Every chaplain in rotation had a tour of two years' incumbency on the Neilgherry Hills. So the scheme, stirred up afresh, was left for my successor to carry out. On my return to duty the scheme was still in abeyance, through the divergent opinions of the Building Committee. A few days after my arrival, however, the bishop came on visitation, bringing with him the last plan designed by the Government architect.

The Church Building Committee was called together, and the plan submitted, and seemed at one time likely to share the fate of three former ones, which the Committee in their collective wisdom had rejected.

One member, an old general, who had a mania for bungalow building, and had erected a small town, stoutly stood out for simply enclosing the ground with a *wall*, and leaving the church to a future generation.

Another member thought the plan too elaborate, and savouring of popery in disguise.

Another thought four walls of brick and mortar, with a roof, sufficient to worship God in.

The good common-sense of the bishop came to the rescue. His lordship thought the time had arrived when churches might be erected in his diocese with greater regard to ecclesiastical propriety. His lordship thought the design a fitting one.

My friends of the Committee, thus hard pushed, did not like to oppose the diocesan; but a brilliant thought occurred to one of them.

Who was to pay for the plan?

Forty pounds, out of sixty or seventy only in the bank!

I accepted the responsibility of collecting this money, reassumed the secretaryship on the understanding that I was to be permitted to commence operations at once; and the meeting broke up.

One of my parishioners, with experience in building, had offered his services to superintend, for the love of the work; and so we recommenced our labours.

The following day the lines of the foundations were traced out, and a band of Wudders (people accustomed to earthwork), pick in hand, were busily engaged digging the trenches.

The estimated cost of the building, without any interior fittings, was estimated at 10,000 rupees.

Having no contractors to deal with (beyond those supplying foundation stones and chunam or mortar), we were able to build when we had money, and stop when the funds ceased.

When my scaffolding of bamboos was

raised, and people perceived that we were in earnest, funds began to pour in, but the amount to be raised was large.

The architect had sent a pretty sketch of the church as it would appear when completed. This I had photographed and placed at the head of a subscription card, and given to collectors wherever I had friends in India.

We had some valuable gifts.

The Principal of Cooper's Hill College presented a beautiful western rose window, to the memory of a beloved child. Altar, vestments for it, pulpit, font, reading-desk, communion-plate, and altar cross quickly followed.

The shell of the building was completed for 8000 rupees, that is, 200*l.* under the estimated cost.

The next step was consecration. The bishop was in England on sick leave.

Fortunately, Bishop Milman was on a tour of visitation at the time, and kindly promised, on his way to the "Blue Mountains, the Neilgherry Hills," to visit Bangalore, and consecrate the building for us.

This he promised with his usual beautiful self-denial whenever work was to be accomplished, more especially his MASTER's work, for it sadly curtailed his visit to the Neilgherries, where he had hoped for a *little* rest.

The church was built and consecrated, but where was the parson?

It had been erected by private enterprise to meet a want of the district. Government had given no aid whatever towards its erection, and so the Church Building Committee had the matter entirely in their own hands.

They considerately left the disposal of the incumbency in my hands. So I proceeded with the task.

It had always been understood, that when the church should be erected, the duty of serving it should first be offered to a clergyman who, travelling at the expense of Government, relieved the chaplains of much of their out-station duty.

He was available to assist them at any time when they were compelled, which was only once every quarter, to be absent. To this gentleman, then, the incumbency was primarily offered—the compliment acknowledged, and declined.

Now was the opportunity for daily services, weekly Eucharists, and a fitting ritual.

During my tour on the hills (of which, to give the history of " All Saints," Bangalore, I have for the present omitted all mention) I became acquainted with the Rev. Dr. Pope, who had a college there, and assisted the chaplain also.

On my return to Bangalore, and the completion of the church, I found myself in communication with him about the wardenship of Bishop Cotton's school and college.

He was not willing to accept the appointment without some definite clerical work, and here the opportunity presented itself.

The result was all that could be desired. Daily services were instituted, the boarders of the college, formed the choir, and for many months the services were celebrated purely for the love of the work. At last Government, shamed into action, gave a tardy annual honorarium to the priest in charge.

He was a scholar and divine, and had for his literary abilities and missionary work, obtained the title of D.D. from the University of Oxford.

And thus, All Saints, Bangalore was built AD MAJOREM DEI GLORIAM.

My attention was next turned to laying out and beautifying the general cemetery, the site of which had been chosen in my district; this spot was destined to be further hallowed to me by its becoming the resting-place of my dear wife and eldest child.

In narrating the history of "All Saints," I have been compelled to anticipate some portion of my work as chaplain, so we will proceed to the Neilgherry Hills, the "Blue Mountains" of the South of India, and to Ootacamund, its chief station, to which I was appointed.

We travelled by rail and transit until the foot of the ghaut was reached, at a place called *Kolar*.

Here we changed our mode of conveyance and took to *tonjons* or *muncheels*. The *tonjon* was a species of heavy chair with sides and a top to it, hung on a pole fastened into a socket, back and front. The *muncheel* was a hammock slung on a pole with a canvas-frame top, movable, to keep off the sun.

A gradual ascent of more than 7000 feet taxed to the uttermost the endurance of the bearers, a diminutive race of men, all muscle.

Their song we found quite different to the song of the bearers in the plains, though it bore a family resemblance and retained the metal ring of voice.

Ascending, new beauties of scenery constantly arrested the attention, a panorama of delight, after the hot, dusty, and sweltering lowland.

On the right was the huge rock with its great clefts, with here and there a tree fern putting forth its six feet fronds, cascades of sparkling water pouring down in grateful streams, and on the left was a huge precipice several hundred feet in depth, clothed with ferns and coffee plants bearing their scarlet berries.

How delightful it was to watch the change

of vegetation as you ascended, breathing a cooler atmosphere at every step.

At the commencement of the ghaut, the chief objects were cocoa-nut, betel, palms and plantains, to be succeeded by wild roses, honeysuckle, and geraniums growing with lavish prodigality.

We arrived first at Coonoor, situated on the top of the ghaut of the same name. There is an excellent hotel here with a specimen of *heliotrope*, fifteen feet in height, and proportionately broad.

It possesses a neat little church, with a most beautifully kept churchyard. The station itself presents the appearance of a number of hills all studded with picturesque bungalows, looking like Swiss châlets.

Having three months' " privilege leave," we remained at this station for two, and then moved to Ootacamund (or Ooty, as it is called), a distance of twelve miles.

The station is situated on gently undulating hills; on the sides of which, as at Coonoor, mansionlike-looking bungalows, are dotted about here and there.

The climate of Ooty, during the month of May, resembles that of April in England;

SHOLA.

the sun's rays, however, are much more powerful, and after 8 a.m. unpleasantly warm. The thermometer stands at about

60° in the shade throughout the day; and out-door exercise is at all times pleasant and beneficial.

There are well-made roads, winding round the foot of the hills, and bridle-paths, which give an endless variety of views to the various places of interest all around.

The " sholas," which are small patches of forest in the gorges between the hills, down which streams of water flow into a boulder bed at the bottom, covered with ferns of every description, are very pleasing to the eye.

In those " sholas " are endless companies of huge black monkeys with white beards.

The sides of the precipices, or *kuds*, as they are termed, are clothed with a variety of forest-trees, indigenous to the hills, most of them very old, and the mossy branches of many laden with ferns and orchids.

The rhododendron flourishes in abundance, the arbutus, wild raspberry, blackberry, and bilberry shrubs also abound.

Banks of soft green moss, wild straw-berries and violets spread over the slopes, with occasionally a lovely bank of maiden-hair fern.

At the sides of the road may be seen, in profusion, the wild geranium, blue and white iris, white and pink wild roses, honeysuckle, and the golden yellow blossom of the furze or gorse.

In the public gardens at Ooty, numerous kinds of flowers flourish and spread in a manner unknown at home, hedges of fuchsias and heliotropes, covered with blossom.

The oak, ivy, heath, box, dahlia, verbena, calceolaria, foxglove, and others, too numerous to mention here, abound; and, of late years, the chinchona-tree has been most successfully cultivated.

Those who desire to enjoy the climate and scenery of the Neilgherries, should visit them, it is said, before the month of June, or after September. The rains set in early in the former month, and then thick white clouds of mist obscure the views, and detract much from the pleasure of out-door exercise.

To the lovers of ornithology, the hills present a perfect paradise of enjoyment.

" Passing, over the 'sparrow,' and the
' carrion crow ' (for the smaller crow of the
plains, with ashy grey neck and breast, has
not yet found his way up the ghauts), we
find the lovely ' myna' (a starling), with
his jet-black plumage and golden wattles.

" Then comes the red-whiskered bul-bul,
with his black head and crest, crimson
whiskers, light hair-brown plumage, cheerily
sending forth his notes on a hideous tuft of
wild tobacco plant.

" Then follow the 'grey tit,' the 'white-
eyed flower-pecker.'

" Then again, though so small—only four
inches in length—we find the ' Neilgherry
flower-pecker,' hunting as busily as possible
for insects. The ' butcher-bird,' the ' black
robin,' the ' skylark,' all come in order.

" Then what is that running across your
path : mice ?

" No. It is the ' painted bush quail,' which
you will not obtain on the plains.

" Then you may see the ' Neilgherry black-
bird' very like its European brother, and
" the blue rock thrush ' supposed from its

solitary habits to be the 'swallow of the Holy Scriptures, that sitteth alone on the housetop.'

"These are not all. There is the 'laughing thrush,' the 'blue-necked bee-eater,' the 'green barbet,' and the 'Hoopoe,' with his large crest, long curved beak, and quaintly banded plumage."

But we must pass on from birds to men.

In our walks we often came across a lovely open space with grass so closely cropped and so fine, as to form a perfect carpet of velvet-like moss.

Here one stumbles upon a hut, in the shape of a straw-skep or the tilt of a waggon, and near it stands a Toda or Tuda. He is described as a fine, tall, athletic-looking fellow, with an open, expressive, and ingenuous countenance. A large full eye, a Roman nose, and fine teeth. He has no covering upon his head, wearing his hair six or seven inches long, parted from the centre, and forming natural bushy circlets all round.

His costume is simple enough, formed of

a short garment round the waist, fastened by a girdle, with an upper mantle or blanket that covers the whole person, except the head, legs, and right arm.

Near him stands, looking with all her dark eyes, his wife, the pattern of a "pretty Jewess."

She has a pleasing and feminine expression of countenance, and is distinguished by her fine form of person, and her beautiful black long tresses, which flow in unrestrained luxuriance on her neck and shoulders. Her dress is similar to that of the man, but covers the whole person.

The "Todas," called Todan individually, do not congregate in villages but live apart, there not being generally more than four or five habitations together.

Colonel Marshall, in his clever and interesting book, "A Phrenologist amongst the Todas," says of them, "there is much of the blameless Ethiopian about them, and something of the Jew and of the Chaldean in their appearance. The voice of the men is grave and sedate, and that of the women

musical and refined; the latter arising from
the gentleness of their disposition.   They

TODA SALUTATION.

salute by raising the thumb edge of the
right hand vertically to the nose and forehead.   A second salutation, called *Ada-*

buddiken, is very singular, as shown in the illustration."

They are a pastoral people, living a most Arcadian life, breed no animals but the "buffalo," and exist on milk and grain.

They possess no knowledge of the Hindu religion. They regard the sun and moon as gods. Their belief is that they and their cattle are born out of the earth. When they die they go to *Amnor,* their heaven, where the buffaloes join them to supply milk. They have sacred groves, a priest who is supported by tithes, which he returns in prayers and religious services.

Colonel Marshall gives a beautiful description of the land they live in. "Picture," he says," an abrupt-edged table-land on the apex of a solitary mountain—a very Laputa in its complete isolation of some 7000 feet in altitude—whose evergreen surface is one continued intermixture of rounded hills, with tracts of rolling prairie; the hills as accessible as those of Malvern, the prairie-land as ceaseless in its long undulations as the billows of an ocean. Short, coarse grass clothes the whole, save where the deep forest holds possession of the damp secluded valleys, or the cool little woods moss the banks of the prolonged gulleys through which the trickling streams course down the hill-sides, then collect, and through successive vigorous rapids and tumultuous cataracts, precipitate themselves into the plain below. The grass in spots is covered with wild flowers. Climbers in great variety of grace and form swing in festoons from the limbs of the gnarled old forest-trees, bearded with lichen or ornamented with varieties of flowing orchids, which cling to the branches of the moss-covered timber. In the dark secluded shades a great variety of ferns, from the fern-tree to those of the smallest size, grace the gloom.

> ' O, might I here
> In solitude live savage, in some glade
> Obscured, where highest woods impenetrable
> To star or sunlight, spread their umbrage broad.' "

Their temples are conical in form, covered with thatch, and surmounted with a stone about a foot in diameter, as shown in the illustration.

They are the very reverse of the Turks, for

SACRED TEMPLE, TODA.

the women enjoy a plurality of husbands. She may have two or three, with whom she takes up her abode in succession, remaining a month or two with each as the case may be. The man is allowed only one wife.

A few words respecting the funeral cere-

monies of this peculiar people will be of
interest, and are best given in the words of
the Rev. P. Perceval :—

" The funeral rites of the Todas," he says,
" are peculiar. When it is evident the sick
person must soon die, near relatives ask
what may be his dying wishes; then, among
other matters, he names certain buffaloes
which he desires may accompany him. The
body is kept there three or four days, to allow
time for the requisite preparations. Fasting,
cutting off the hair, putting off ornaments,
chanting morning and evening laments,
mutual condolence, falling on the corpse,
with other expressions of grief, are observed
on the death of a Toda. On the day appointed for the burning of the body, a bier is
prepared of boughs of trees, on which the
body is laid, dressed in a new garment and
mantle, and wearing the ornaments the deceased had been accustomed to. The body
is borne along, followed by the mourners,
male and female, chanting the lament, and
after these a multitude follows, bearing
bundles of wood for the pyre and small sacks

of grain, cups made of leaves, filled with milk variously prepared, and butter with cooking utensils. At a distance a herd of buffaloes moves along, intended for the obsequies. The bier is put down at a little distance from the place of burning, when the friends and

MOURNING.

relations take up earth, and with much ceremony sprinkle it on the body, and seating themselves around, continue their lament. The illustration shows the form of this mourning.

"The funeral obsequies are accompanied

by the sacrifice of a number of milch buffaloes, which are formed into a circle round the body and there slain; and as each of the victims falls, the deceased is addressed by the party sacrificing, who mentions the name of the animal, saying it is sent to accompany him."

Let us now go in and see who live in the station itself, for it is a civil and not a military one.

With the exception of a few executive officers, the residents for the most part were retired officers, who at that time purposed spending the remainder of their lives in, to them, this earthly paradise, on their pensions and off-reckonings.

I found the church services weary in the extreme. I took much pains with the choir, the "Islington" hymns disappeared, and the "Ancient and Modern" took their place with their music. Frequent celebrations of the Holy Communion and numerous services followed, and which have been maintained ever since.

Meantime, for many, many months, I

endured the obloquy of all pioneers in such works of progress, to see, however, as years passed away and passions calmed down, the fruit of much endurance. I had the pleasure of being libelled in two weekly papers for many months, for it was quite impossible that any good thing could emanate from a source rejected in the holy circles of Madras from the very first.

When I left my charge, I had the pleasure of receiving a handsome testimonial of the affection of the people.

We parted after all with much regret, and the times are even now discussed by a few old residents with affectionate regard for the Padre who had infused new life into dead bones.

CHAPTER XI.

" Still from one sorrow to another thrown."—ANON.
" Each cross hath its inscription."—PROVERB.

ON our return to Bangalore the pensioners' church had to be built, an account of which I have already detailed, much other work supplemented and supervised, and the ordinary routine carried on. I was' pleased to return to my old charge, and my people scemed equally gratified. So the life was very pleasant, alas, not to endure long!

After sixteen years of unalloyed domestic happiness, the "desire of mine eyes," the partner of all my joys and sorrows, the participator and encourager of all my pastoral work was to be removed to her rest, in twelve short hours. Thus a second time had I prepared and beautified "God's acre" for the reception of my beloved. Though recruited somewhat by my tour on the hills, this great sorrow, added to many years of incessant work, entirely prostrated me.

God had spared me five of my children; with these as a prey in my hand must I return to my native country. Fearing, however, the winter season for them, I plodded on to work out the time with heavy heart. My eldest child, with wonderful force of character, became a second mother to the younger children, and supported me in my sorrow with loving devotion.

Our passage was taken and our goods and chattels put up to auction, when a fever seized her, and in three days she joined her sweet mother, with these words on her lips,—

> "Only, O Lord, in Thy dear love
> Fit us for perfect rest above."

Alas!

> "Oh! who that ever heard that dying strain
> Could think to mingle in the world again!"

We hurried on board: yes, indeed; but, as Thackeray says, "Love seems to survive life, and to reach beyond it. I think we take it with us past the grave.

"Do not we give it still to those who have left us?

"May we not hope that they feel it for us, and that we shall leave it here in one or two fond bosoms when we also are gone."

We are on board one of the P. and O. steamers with two of our native servants, an ayah and a butler, the former of whom had been with us for fifteen years.

How amusing it was to see them in our English house on first arrival, creeping up the stairs on all-fours, feeling quite bewildered with a succession of steps, so unlike the few flights of stairs seen in most parts of India.

After an absence of sixteen years how terribly sad was the realization of the removal of some of the most loved faces, and which distance had seemed to shroud from the memory.

How great a joy, too, was the "daily service," and a church open at all times for private devotions.

I gladly helped some of my overworked brethren, and at one time took six weeks' duty at a public cemetery.

The chaplain was on the eve of a breakdown; there was no one to help him, and he was too poor to remunerate any one, when I stepped into the gap.

And what a gap! There were two chaplains, of whom I was now to form one; and in six weeks, with no special mortality, we buried three hundred people.

Morning duty one day from nine a.m. to one p.m., the next day from two p.m. to five p.m.

How sad it was, and my own heart surcharged with a double grief. I tried by enunciating all the hope the lovely service expresses to infuse that blessed hope into their sorrow-laden hearts, and not without success in many instances, as their thanks evidenced.

But it is in our saddest moods sometimes that external circumstances affect us in their most ludicrous aspects. And so it was here.

I had a real " Bumble " to attend upon me.

He had been a butcher, he informed me, and showed me in proof of his assertion his scarred hands.

He was also a poet, though his poetry, I confess, did not strike me as of a high order; many generations I thought might safely pass away ere Royalty dubbed him " Poet Laureate."

This man was the very essence of officialism. One day the chapel-keeper had mounted a ladder to correct the clock, when out rushed " Bumble," college cap on head, gown well-betagged in disorder, crying, " STOP! STOP! The clock must be wound up OFFICIALLY. I will REPORT it."

The chaplain met the bodies at the entrance of the chapel, repeated the opening sentences to each arrival until the chapel was full, and then read the service.

Who can describe the fetid state of the atmosphere on a hot day! The least sensitive person could not fail being nauseated. And then the procession to the grave—grave after grave, all over the cemetery—no little exertion; then the hurrying back to the chapel, to receive another ghastly instalment.

I became great friends with the undertakers, who frequently entered into confidential communications with me on the subject of their profession.

One day one of my friends thus addressed me,—

" *Nice thing, sir,* next Wednesday ! "
" *Indeed,*" I replied. " *Yes, sir,* LEADEN COFFIN AND FITTINGS."

" Pray, what are ' fittings' ? " I inquired. " Oh, sir, fittings are the plumes, and the scarves, and the wands "—with a graceful wave of his arm and his eyes sparkling.

I tried hard to get out of my friend what

profit would accrue to him for the " *leaden coffin and fittings,*" but he was too wrapt in their glory to give heed to my query, or resolute on an absolute silence; so I passed on, and buried my pauper brother or sister *midst many reflections.*

A few months and I must return to duty in the East.

I hired and furnished a house in the neighbourhood of a good school. I had a good deal of travelling about at this time, and one peculiar adventure may interest the reader.

Two incidents occurred to me in one day. I was travelling by slow train to Oxford to meet a fast one for London. The air was raw and chilly; it was toward evening, and a drizzling rain was falling. Third class was my carriage, and altogether I did not feel very comfortable; when I found my innermost thoughts given expression to by a traveller, a labouring man, entering my compartment with a " *Ugh! What a climate this is !* "

I asked, " Pray in what other climate have you been ? " He replied, " *India.*" This led to general conversation, and I found I had visited the station where he had been quartered as a soldier.

The train, which was a slow one, just at this juncture went off at a prodigious speed, when I said in an encouraging tone to my companion, "*Ah! we are getting along now.*" "*Yes, sir. The* MAIL *is behind us.*" I was glad to find myself at Oxford with unbroken bones.

When nearing Oxford he left the train, and making me a salute, said, "Might I take the liberty of shaking hands with you?" "Certainly, my friend," and so we parted; he was eking out his pension by doing odd jobs of gardening.

"Look sharp! Three minutes to change your train. The iron horse is snorting, impatient of delay." A general rush, and I found myself in a carriage containing four men and a boy.

My entrance was evidently far from welcome, as I was immediately addressed with these words, "This is a *smoking* carriage." I did not take any notice; when the same individual said, "Perhaps, sir, you don't *know* that this is a SMOKING carriage?"

"Thank you," I replied; "I am going to smoke."

I did not at all admire the look of these people, but I buttoned up my coat securely.

I then took from my cigar case a Trichinopoly cheroot, and withdrawing the reed commenced smoking. This novel-looking kind of firework attracted their attention, and led afterwards to a little communication, which resulted in the conversation I am about to narrate, and which, had it not actually occurred, I should have placed to the credit of an ardent imagination.

The four men each occupied a corner of the carriage, whilst exactly opposite to me a boy reclined, trying evidently to get some sleep. Meanwhile I was not a little amused at the manner in which time was passed by my companions.

A little old man in one corner, who was addressed as *Peter*, amused himself by humming operatic tunes in a falsetto key.

A fat man, evidently the father of the reclining lad, kept trying to induce him to take a pull from a black bottle, which from its odour I imagined to be gin, to wash down the more substantial fragments of a pork pie.

The boy evidently wished to " rest, and be thankful," and resented the ill-timed efforts of his affectionate parent by kicking out at him and saying, " *Can't you leave a feller alone ?* " The other men amused themselves with giving and taking odds on some forth-coming race.

Meantime the men became more friendly towards the intruding stranger, and at last quite confiding.

Mitis—" *This Macilente, Signior, begins to be more sociable on a sudden.*"

Whether my rubicund appearance struck them,

> " The man of health,
> Complexionally pleasant,"

I cannot say, but at last one of them said to me,—

Q

" Now I will tell you something to do you *good*. When you get up in the morning, and the coppers is hot, just take a soda and milk, half soda-water you know and half milk, and a biscuit. I always does, and I gives my missus half. It is wonderful how it picks you up."

He might have lived in the days of Goldsmith, who wrote :—

" Here, waiter, more wine ! let me sit while I'm able,
  Till all my companions sink under the table."

He then gave me a sketch of some of his country expeditions.

" I gives my missus a *outing* sometimes," he said, " and then we goes to *Hepsom*. We have two rooms for half-a-crown a day ; and when you gets up in the morning and takes a walk on them *Downs*, and sees them ʜoaks, that is what I call the beautifullest sight in natur'. There is nothing like them *Hepsom Downs* to my mind."

" Oh, no ! " says *Peter*, " that's not the beautifullest thing. You just go to *Good*wooᴅ *Race Coorse*, and get on the *Good*wooᴅ Race

Stand, and look round; that is the beautiful-lest sight in natur', I say."

Peter's word was *infallible,* and so the argument ceased.

The next scene came from the fat man, who dives under the seat, and uncovers a cock with a bleeding comb, trimmed, I fancy, for fighting.

He held the poor bird up to me, and said, " Ain't he a beauty ? Now what do you think he's worth ? "

I pleaded my ignorance; when he continued, " Well, he's worth a five pun note. But I will show you another." Diving under the seat again, he produced a hen. " Now don't you call *her* a beauty: what do you think she's worth ? Why she's worth a ten pun note. She's a rare un to lay." With which expression of opinion he tied her up in a pocket handkerchief, and restored her to her basket under the seat.

There were then various altercations regarding the winning horses in certain races, determined by the scrutiny of a daily racing calendar, well thumbed.

We were now rapidly approaching our journey's end. There were various bets on the time of our arrival, and the possibility of their being in time for a train by the underground line; and then a conversation carried on in an undertone, the subject of which was an appointment at some gambling-hell.

The two young men were to go in at different times; and one, as looking the more innocent—on which his companion rallied him —to pretend to be ignorant of certain racing issues, and give his companion a lead. And thus they devised their evil deeds.

The train stopped, and they went their evil way to carry them into execution.

God assoil them! When will the Church be able to reach such men, and bring them to a better mind!

I had now to think and prepare for my return to India, to complete my time for pension.

I visited my old parish in Norfolk, to find the children whom I had left, fathers of families; and on the whole very few, comparatively speaking, had died out.

How different would have been the issue in India, removed to other stations, or by death! Scarcely one would have remained.

During my furlough I had taken a good deal of duty in town and country. All matters ecclesiastical had wonderfully progressed in the former; and the co-operation of Priest and Layman was very striking. In the latter, schools had been built, churches restored, but the services were very much on the same level as when I quitted England for the first time.

Indeed prayers were read out of books which had been in use for generations, and I found myself several times on the point of praying for good Queen Anne, instead of good Queen Victoria.

The underground railways were a new feature, and so also appeared the hurry and bustle of men, jostling one another, with the lines of anxiety depicted on their countenances; which puzzled me much, especially as I reflected that another train would be due in three minutes.

Then again, in London, the old familiar

thoroughfares so much altered for the better, and frequently recognizable only by the sight of a building left here and there of old memory.

The parks seemed to preserve their identity the best, though greatly beautified.

The horses seemed to me, after the Eastern Arab, gigantic.

In the shops a restless competition seemed active, and very far from being strictly honest.

However, time passed away, and the sad hour of leave-taking with my children came.

My youngest child, for hours before my departure, would not leave me for an instant; and to part with the baby-boy wrenched the heart as those only know who have had thus to suffer.

> "As we love our youngest children best,
>   So the last fruit of our affection,
>   Wherever we bestow it, is most strong;
>   Since 'tis indeed our latest harvest-home,
>   Last merriment 'fore winter."

As I was unencumbered, I determined to go *via* the Continent, and join the " P. and O." steamer at Venice.

After ten days' journeying, and visiting Calais, Brussels, crossing the " Brenner Pass," with its cobalt mountains, Insbrück, I reached Munich and Venice—" Beautiful Venice," of all foreign delights the most delightsome.

Here I remained for three days, and then was off to Bombay. Bombay I knew of old, with its splendid harbour and multitudinous assemblage of people.

Then by rail to Madras. I here paid a visit to the Bishop, reporting my arrival. I got permission to visit Bangalore and Ooty, and was at my own request appointed to a small station. It was situated in the South of India, not far from " Cape Comorin." I anticipated much pleasure in seeing a part of the country which would be quite new to me, and in this I was not disappointed.

In Bangalore I met with my old butler, who joined his fortunes to mine, so we journeyed by rail through the Beypore district, and joined the " Backwaters," leading to Quilon, and finally Trevandrum, my headquarters.

Fourteen principal rivers take their rise in mountains which form the background of the territory of Travancore. These form inland lakes, which, united by canals, form means of water communication between the northern and southern districts.

These are traversed by means of a species of canoe, or " dug out " as it is called, made out of a single tree, with a covering of cadjans, or palmyra leaves, fastened to a framework of bamboo. Sometimes by jungars, that is, two canoes lashed together, and joined by a platform of wood and a covering. And by means of cabin boats, a large boat containing twelve to sixteen rowers, with a cabin-like covering at the stern.

Travancore is termed by the natives " The land of charity," from its fertility, the agriculturists raising sometimes three crops of rice in the same year. A fertility which reminds one of what Douglas Jerrold said of Australia—" Earth is so kindly there that, tickle her with a hoe, and she laughs with a harvest."

It has been described as a long narrow

strip of land, running 174 miles, by some thirty to seventy in breadth.

It is backed by mountains rising to 500 feet above the level of the sea. Dense forests cover the uncultivated land, where tigers, elephants, the black cheetah, or leopard, and the ordinary cheetah, abound.

The hill slopes are planted with the "Jack-tree" (*Artocarpus*), which yields a yellow wood, most useful for the manufacture of furniture of every description. The wood is peculiarly yellow when first made up, but after a few months becomes darker, and after a few years very much like mahogany.

The fruit grows to an enormous size, and hangs by a peduncle, first being borne by the branches, then on the trunk, and finally on the roots. The fruit is eaten by the natives; the seeds when roasted and ground make a good flour, and are much prized among the poorer classes.

It is the same with the mango, cashew-nut, and tamarind-trees, nutmegs, cardamums, arrowroot, tapioca, and lemon-grass, all growing in profusion.

The average temperature of Travancore is seventy-eight degrees. The headquarters of the native state is Trevandrum.

Here the Maharajah and the royal family reside. There is a British resident at his Highness's court, an assistant resident, a physician, chaplain, and some few European officers attached to the Nair Brigade. There is a chief engineer and some schoolmasters attached to a college for the education of the natives.

In 1789 Tippoo Saab, son of Hyder Ali, attacked Travancore. Lord Cornwallis came to the rescue, and the result was a treaty, by which the Maharajah agreed to a subsidy, by which troops were maintained, and stationed at Quilon, for the defence of his country.

Quilon was distant forty miles, and I visited it, as my only out-station, once a month. There was a native infantry regiment stationed there officered by Europeans.

It had a large church, and once had been one of the largest of the South Indian garrisons. There was a splendid residency, situated on the banks of the "backwater," which there formed a beautiful lake. It was melancholy to wander over this fine mansion, only occasionally used, by the resident or the chaplain visiting the station. To see the remnants of faded satin furniture, and the old yellow copperplate engravings depicting scenes of bygone events, such as the "Battle of Seringapatam," or the noble features of England's warrior statesmen, such as Warren Hastings, Clive, and Cornwallis, adorning its marble-like walls, made one sigh, and feel that its ancient glories had passed away.

The greater part of the native population of Trevandrum are Brahmins. They wear very little clothing, the upper part of the body and the lower part of the legs being usually bare. They are also distinguished by their caste marks. These are a little dot about the size of a fourpenny piece, or horizontal or perpendicular lines drawn with sacred ashes on the forehead.

If a man wishes to live in the perfect odour of sanctity he rubs the sacred ashes all over the upper part of his body. The perpendicular lines represent a worshipper of *Vishnu*, and the horizontal that of *Siva*.

The women have long, black, luxuriant hair, for the most part very wiry and coarse. This they tie up in knots on the back or on the right side of the head. They are very fond of ornaments, and the Sudra and Shanar women wear cylinders, as earrings, of

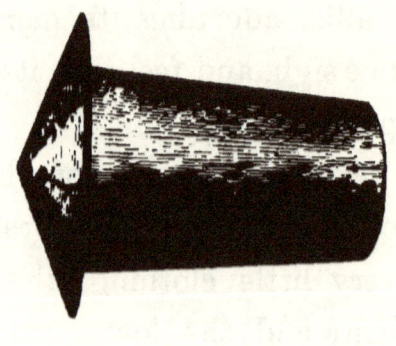

buffalo-horn, weighing more than a quarter of a pound, in each ear. The engraving represents the ear pierced and elongated, for a ring, as worn by the DYAKS, and equally suitable for the buffalo-horn cylinder represented of the TRAVANCOREANS.

This custom of wearing ponderous ear

ornaments prevails also among the Burmese, and is followed by both races. The image of Guadama is always portrayed with long pendent ear-lobes, reaching to his shoulders, evidencing the custom.

Stanley, speaking of some of the South African tribes, says, "they split the lobes of their ears, and introduce such curious things as the necks of gourds or some discs of wood, to extend the gash.

This peculiar custom appears to be a very ancient one, and to be connected with the worship of the sun. Spanish historians mention that elaborate ceremonies were held at the Temple of the Sun at Cuzco on the occasion of boring the ears of the young Peruvian nobles; and that in the cases of princes of the blood, the Inca himself pierced the ear-lobes with a golden pin.

Signor D'Albertis mentions the same custom amongst the inhabitants of New Guinea, he says, "the lobe of their ears is artificially drawn out two or three inches, and often reaches the shoulder." The same custom prevails amongst the Dyaks of Borneo.

And Schweinfurth in his interesting book states that the A-banga and the Monbutto tribes, and the Daika in the Soudan, pierce their ears so that a good thick stick can easily be run through the aperture, and for this purpose the concave portion of the ear is cut out.

Amongst the Travancoreans the method used to admit these ornaments is as follows. The ear is pierced in childhood, and a heavy leaden ring inserted: after a time this is made more weighty, and so at the end of a year or two the fleshy lobe of the ear is dragged down almost to the shoulder.

In the earlier stages the opening is kept clear by a piece of leaf, rolled up tightly so as to form a spring.

They also delight in iron rings, which vary from studs to rings two inches in diameter, fastened through the cartilage of the nose and hanging over the mouth.

Rings are also worn on the second toe of the foot.

With regard to their houses it has been remarked, that " The great ambition of the

Travancoreans, even of the lowest class, is to possess a garden, wherein they can grow with scarcely any trouble or expense the few necessaries of existence.

"Hence a village becomes a series of huts enclosed within gardens, wearing an external verdure and cheerful to the eye."

The enclosures are very neatly kept, the courtyard in front of the house or hut being washed over with wet cowdung, which dries quickly in the sun, and arabesqued with figures or devices drawn in white chalk.

There is usually a well and a shed for cattle, and a cook house; a wooden mortar about three feet in height, with a pestle; a pole shod with iron, for removing the husk of the paddy (rice); and oftentimes a small domestic temple for religious worship in one corner.

In the outside wall is the entrance gateway, with a framework of wood, thatched or tiled, looking very neat, and resembling a small English Lych-gate.

In one small enclosure may be seen grouped together the graceful areca palm, the jack-tree, with the pepper vine climbing up its back, the sago palm, the taliput, besides the cocoa, plantain, tamarind, mango, and coffee-trees.

These gardens are protected by mud or laterite walls, or by hedges of different heights of cactus, and traversed by narrow lanes and by-ways.

The principal inhabitants of Travancore are called Nairs. "They are a mild and very unwarlike people now," says Colonel Drury, "whatever they may have been in times when they were called upon to defend their country."

There is a Nair brigade in Trevandrum, used to guard the entrance to the different palaces and pagodas, and appear as guards of honour in state processions.

They are drilled to a certain point, so as to be able to march in some kind of order, and fire off their muskets without endangering their own lives.

An officer of this brigade told me the following anecdote of one of them.

A private was had up to the orderly-room

for absence from guard ; his excuse pleaded gathering his grain, he had not been a defaulter for eleven years.

It was not a little amusing at times to see these men coming in for duty, with their uniforms tied up in a bundle and carried on their heads.

They are mostly small agriculturists, and receive only a small stipend for their occasional services. The troops, however, for which the Maharajah pays a subsidy to the British Government, are the Indian Sepoys stationed at Quilon.

The most peculiar feature in the domestic life of the Nair is in the institution of marriage.

" The ceremony is performed at an early age by one of the near male relations of the family, usually by a cousin. When the forms attendant on this nominal union have taken place, all communication between them ceases, and the girl returns to her relations. On arriving at or near the age of maturity, a more real ceremony is performed, when another husband presents himself, and this couple now become man and wife; but should the husband after a certain period not be pleased with the lady of his choice, he has the option of returning her to her parents or relatives, and both are free to seek a fresh union in other quarters. No disgrace is attached to this proceeding; nor is the summary divorce and violent disruption of the marriage tie in any way illegal.

"There is in point of fact no actual marriage such as we understand the sacred institution; and it is in consequence of a custom so abhorrent to our feelings of propriety, that in cases of heirdom, either to the Throne or to succession of property, the descent is recognized only in the *female line;* the nephew, not the son, becomes the heir."

To notice another caste, the slave, or Palayan native, is entirely destitute of education, and is considered to be too impure for any one to approach. "In addressing his master, he dare not say I, but *'your slave.'* He dare not call his rice by its ordinary appellation, but *' dirty gruel.'* He asks leave not to take food, but to *' drink water.'*

" His house is called a hut, and his children he speaks of as '*monkeys*' or '*calves ;*' and when speaking he must place his hand over his mouth, lest the breath should go forth and pollute the person whom he is addressing."

The natives of Malabar are all superstitious, from the king on his throne to the poor outcast slave and worshipper of demons.

A black cat seen on a journey, a crow flying across the path, a black lizard falling on any one, a white lizard chirruping, all portend evil, and they will imitate the latter to nullify the effect of the evil omen.

Oftentimes people may be seen suddenly stopping and then turning back; they have received some supposed evil omen, and they must return from whence they came.

There are a host of demons worshipped by the people of Travancore. I will mention a few, and am indebted to a book full of interest on Travancore and its customs, by the Rev. S. Mateer, a London missionary, who for many years has been resident in Travancore.

There is, to begin, " The Demon Mādan, or

he, who is like a cow." This demon is supposed to be of huge proportions, black, and covered with hair like a cow. He is supposed to strike men and oxen with sudden illnesses, and is consequently much dreaded.

There is the "*Furnace Devil*," who is supposed to break the pottery whilst baking in the kiln.

There is the "*Bubble Devil*," who dances on the water. Answering, doubtless, to the "Demon of the Bubbling Well of the Shangaites."

The "*Wicked Devil*" and the "*Fighting Devil*," the latter possibly known to more nations than one.

There is also the "*Giant*," said to be seventeen feet in height, who is revered by the tribes living in the mountains of Travancore.

Another demon is called "*The old man of the three roads*," and is supposed to lurk about where several roads meet, to the fright and injury of passers-by.

And there is "*Little Sattan*," a species of spiteful devil, who throws stones and breaks doors, and puts mud in your food—a kind of Asmodeus, full of quips and oddities.

Some of these demons are supposed to reside in trees, at the foot of which you will see a rude stone set up for image or emblem, on which turmeric or red paint, is daubed. The natives will not pass these in the dark.

Certain days, again, are lucky or the reverse. Tuesdays and Fridays are considered unlucky for many transactions. Some days are considered fortunate for shaving, wearing new clothes, marrying, or undertaking journeys, and oil bathing.

With regard to the latter, all Brahmins bathe daily, but those who can afford an oil bath take it once or twice in the week. It is considered greatly to conduce to health, and is prepared in the following manner.

The oil of the rape seed is prepared by having a great number of medicinal and pungent herbs, particularly the jasmine, steeped in it, and allowed to remain until their virtues are imparted.

They rub it over the head and body, allow it to remain for an hour, and wash it off with water in which the bark of a tree called "Inja" has been steeped, and which then acts as soap.

The ordinary days set apart for this luxury are Wednesdays and Saturdays for men, Tuesdays and Fridays for married women. Monday and Wednesday are set apart for shaving, and Friday for the first wearing a new cloth.

They fully believe in the effects of the "*evil eye*," and procure "mandrums," i.e., prayers written on a leaf, to avert misfortune to a house or property, newly-built or acquired, to be carried on the person, or tied up in the house.

CHAPTER XII.

Leaf-writing—Witchcraft—Doña Juana of Navarre—
Syrian Christians—White Jews—Refugees from
Palestine, A.D. 68—Church and cemetery put in
order—Steadfast little mission—Christians of St.
Thomas—An account of them.

> " Knew many an amulet and charm
> That would do neither good nor harm."
>
> HUDIBRAS.

> " Off! to Thine harvest, Saviour, send
>   The hosts of Thine employ,
> To reap the ripen'd sheaves that bend,
>   And shout them home with joy."
>
> COXE.

IN Travancore, until very recently, all public
documents were written and preserved on
leaves, the leaf used for this purpose being
the *oleah* or *cadjan*, that is, a slip of the
palm leaf.

The natives carry about with them in a

little leathern sheath, a knife, a stylus or pen, and a little instrument with two projections about the eighth of an inch apart for making a circular hole in the leaf, to enable them to tie them together. Thus they always have at hand pen, ink, and paper.

Ink, indeed, they do not want, as the stylus scratches the letters on the dry leaf. They are very expert in its use, and can write as they sit, or walk along the road, leaf in hand.

If they have composed a poem, they will write it on these leaves tied together, and then placing a piece of wood top and bottom, the same shape as the narrow leaf, tie it all up in a bundle; and when requested they will open their book and read, after the same manner as the Prophet Isaiah was read in the synagogue of old.

Most of the Travancoreans place implicit faith in the power of witchcraft. They have recourse to this act as a safe and quiet way of ridding them of an enemy who cannot be openly faced or overcome.

The usual method of proceeding is as follows:—A "*Mandravathy*," or sorcerer, is consulted, who writes a charm or address to some evil spirit. This he does on a cadjan, or on a small sheet of copper, lead, or other metal, which is rolled up as tightly as possible, and placed in an earthen jar or pot, the aperture of which might be about an inch and a half in diameter, or else in an empty cocoa-nut shell.

This contains also the skull of a black cat, sometimes a bat's head, and a wooden figure or doll made of cloth, or, again, wet rice flour, meant to represent the figure of the party to be injured.

The figure will have three or four nails or pins driven into it, at the places indicating the parts of the body to be attacked with disease.

This is designed to cause the enemy torture or suffering in these parts, similar to what he would have endured had they been actually thrust into his living body.

The effect is supposed to be produced after the jar has been buried in the ground. The spot usually selected is at the threshold over which the victim has to step.

Sometimes I have known it buried in the floor of the cook-room, and have one in my possession thence obtained.

From the time of his stepping over the figure, his sufferings are supposed to commence.

Another method of "jar do your duty," is to place it on their "*homum*," or sacrificial altar, the fire being sustained with ghee (clarified butter), and unceasing invocations made to the demon whose aid is sought.

More enlightened natives do not believe that death will ensue, but fully trust in sickness following, provided the curse is properly prepared by persons whose lives have been devoted to such acts.

There is a curious passage in Mr. Hepworth Dixon's "Royal Windsor," a veritable counterpart in the fifteenth century of that which is enacting in the nineteenth in Travancore.

He writes, " Doña Juana, of Navarre, calling in her secret agents, Roger Cottes and Petronel Brocard, requested them to study with her how to wither or destroy the king by means of sorcery.

" Father Randolf, her confessor, was engaged to help them, by his skill as a divine, in making compacts with the powers of darkness.

" Figures of the king were shaped by witch and sorcerer ; figures of wax, which being cursed by spells, were pierced by many pieces, and set in a warm place to melt. ' As they dissolve and perish, even so shall he dissolve and perish,' ran the incantation."

So we are not so very much better than our neighbours, when royalty itself in the beginning of the fifteenth century could devise such witcheries and believe in them !

The authoress of " At Home in Fiji " has a passage in her interesting book on this subject, which deals not only with witchcraft in Fiji, but also in the British Isles !

She writes :—" A person having a grudge against his neighbour, will try to obtain something which he has touched—a bit of his dress, the refuse of his food, or, above all, a piece of his hair—and, having uttered certain charmed words, will conceal this about the house, generally in the thatch, with a conviction that ere long the victim will waste away.

" These superstitions are almost identical with those so common in the British Isles, and which still perhaps linger there.

" Thus, the police records have recently reported cases in which waxen images have been moulded to represent persons, against whom some miscreant had a grudge.

" So late as 1870, at Beauly in Scotland, a man was proved to have made an image of clay, which he buried near the house of a farmer to whom he owed a grudge, fully believing that as the rain washed away the clay so his enemy would pine and die.

" And in the same district a woman was found sticking lumps of mud on the trees with the same object.

" In 1872, two onions, stuck full of pins and ticketed with the name of the intended victim, were found hidden in a chimney corner in Somerset."

Amongst the Travancoreans were large numbers of Syrian Christians, or Christians of St. Thomas; of these I shall have to speak further on, when narrating my work in this station.

Another set of people also I met with occasionally, the "White Jews." Those I saw were very well off, striking in appearance, bearing all the features of the Jew, with a pale yellowish complexion.

There is a colony of them residing in Cochin, apart by themselves in the midst of the native population. They number about 300. For the most part they are very poor. According to their own statements, they are refugees from Palestine A.D. 68, when, they say, 10,000 of them settled on the Malabar coast. Probably, it has been remarked, 1000 would be nearer the truth.

A full account of them is to be found in "Buchanan," who made many successful discoveries of Syriac and Hebrew MSS. of the Pentateuch, which are now preserved in the Cambridge University Library.

Having now given a sketch of the native population, with some account of their more peculiar manners and customs, amongst whom I was now to reside, I will pass on to describe my work.

My first duty, after having made myself

acquainted with my people, was to put my church in decent and reverent order. And this it needed sadly. It was a pretty little Gothic church, much more ecclesiastical in its outward appearance than most churches at that time in India.

Government build, or build in part, furnish, and keep in repair, the churches which are required for the use of their servants, whether military or civil.

I applied to Government, who gave me a grant of 140*l.*, with which I made the sacred building decent.

The church consisted of nave, tower, and two small transepts, used respectively for baptistery and vestry.

The cemetery was in wild disorder; but a band of convicts for levelling and path-making, and a few gardeners, and the place was made a " pleasant spot."

One side of the cemetery ran alongside the public road; and the presence of convicts digging trenches alongside the paths, made the natives think the Padre was very busy in drain-making.

They were much delighted when in the place of drains, as they had imagined, they found every variety of beautiful flower and shrub.

Soon after it was finished, I was stopped on the road by an old Brahmin, who told me he had watched the improvement, and that for such care I should certainly have God's blessing.

The church was opened for Sunday and weekday services, and was put at the service of a small Church of England Mission.

I found the mission in a very languishing state; and yet with fluctuating fortunes, according as to whom the chaplain for the time being happened to be, it had existed for more than forty years.

Though persistently assailed on the right hand by the Romanists, and on the left by the London Mission, they had steadfastly kept true to the Catholic Church of England,

I could expect, as I soon found, no countenance from my ecclesiastical superior, and so set to work to do what I could in faith.

1 found an aged catechist, an old man of

very good parts and a born poet, but too infirm to keep the people together, or conduct the services as they should be conducted.

I was fortunate in obtaining a young and zealous man named Matthew, who worked acceptably, and added much "to the Church."

All sacramental services I celebrated for them myself by means of the catechist as an interpreter.

I was much struck on this, and on all occasions of attending divine service with a native congregation, at their rapt and reverent attention to their reader and preacher.

All native pastors with whom I have become acquainted preached fluently and without the slightest apparent embarrassment.

At times when the preacher was dwelling with fervour on the glad tidings and proclaiming the Saviour of Mankind, he would pause and ask them a question, when a hum of assent would burst forth, showing their heartfelt attention.

Not less striking are the questions of those inquiring for the first time, "how to be saved," and the strange light in which many facts stated in the Holy Gospels appear to them.

It was no work of languor or indifference with this little body of Christians, but a soul-stirring matter, which it behoved them to know and assure themselves of, beyond all other questions which had ever arrested their attention.

After my arrival, and during the time the Maharajah's college was open, there was a great influx to my English and native congregations. This arose from the "Syrian Christians, or Christians of St. Thomas," residing in Trevandrum for the purpose of education.

I held a class of them for the purpose of teaching the distinctive doctrines of the English Church, and I have little doubt that many will ere long join her communion.

And here it may be interesting to many to say a few words about the Syrian Christians, much of which I have gathered from an article published in the *Bombay Gazette* many years ago.

" The Christians of St. Thomas, and their Liturgies," was the title of the book reviewed, and written by the Rev. G. B. Howard, a Madras chaplain.

" It is almost impossible to doubt," says the reviewer, " that the Church of Malabar was originally founded by the Apostle Thomas, who afterwards lost his life at Madras, so strong is the evidence in favour of the tradition which is brought forward by Mr. Howard."

Claudius Buchanan was of this opinion, and it is supported by the local tradition both of Christians and Jews.

That St. Thomas ended his days in India is certain from the testimony of the European historians, and was notoriously well-known in Europe 1500 years ago ; and the belief of the inhabitants of the Carnatic is sufficient to fix the locality of his death with tolerable certainty.

It must be remembered that the difficulties of access to the South of India in ancient times were very trifling compared with what they afterwards became in the troubled ages that succeeded; and a constant stream of commerce was kept up between Southern Asia and the Levant.

Large colonies of Jews also existed in the country, and it was from among them that the Apostle made his first converts.

A journey from Jerusalem to Trevandrum or Wailapoor, in those days, was probably not at all more difficult than it would be now, though it may have taken rather longer to achieve.

It appears that St. Thomas having founded the Malabar Church, crossed over to the Eastern coast, and preached the Gospel on that side. Here he incurred the enmity of the Brahmins, and was put to death in a popular tumult on the spot now known as "St. Thomas's Mount," near Madras.

His remains have since been removed by the Portuguese to Goa, where they may still be seen.

The Malabar Church, nevertheless, spread and flourished, and intercourse with the West was still kept up for some time.

Amongst the subscriptions to the decrees

of Nice, A.D. 325, is the signature of John, Metropolitan of Persia and India.

In the sixth century an Alexandrian merchant, named Cosmos, thus describes Malabar :—

"In the Malabar country also, where pepper grows, there are Christians; and in Culliana (Quilon), as they call it, there is a bishop, who comes from Persia, where he is consecrated. Lastly, our King Alfred, according to the testimony of the 'Saxon Chronicle,' and of William of Malmesbury, despatched Swithelm, Bishop of Sherborne, on a mission of congratulation, with presents, to this distant country.

"Swithelm performed his long and dangerous embassy with success, and returned to England laden with precious gifts and spices.

"Marco Polo, in the thirteenth century, visited the scene of the martyrdom of the Apostle, and declares that it was frequented by many Christians and Saracen pilgrims; and when Vasco de Gama arrived in 1448, he found in India a people who had professed the Christian faith for many generations."

A few more particulars will suffice, and bring us up to the present date.

In 1595 Alexis de Menezes was sent as archbishop to Goa. He received instructions from Pope Clement VIII. to inquire into the faith of the Syrian bishop and his flock. There was a Synod held at Diamper, near Cochin, in 1599; here decrees were passed, confirming the doctrines of Rome, and repudiating those hitherto held by the Syrian Church.

This continued for about fifty years, when the Syrians revolted from Rome and appointed their archdeacon as metropolitan.

In this way arose the two great bodies which now exist. The Syrians (called also Nazarenes, and by Europeans " The Christians of St. Thomas," really " The Syrian Christians of Malabar) and the Romo-Syrians.

In 1854 the latter numbered 81,886, and the former 109,123. They have about 156 churches and between 800 and 900 priests. They are governed by a metropolitan bishop, and the priests are called " Cattanas." The last census, 1875, gives the following numbers in Travancore:—111,155 Roman Catholics, 61,593 Protestants, and 295,770 Syrians, the latter number representing the Syrians proper. They have the threefold ministry.

The churches are solid structures with a huge frontage, long and narrow, with gable ends surmounted by the cross. The walls are supported by buttresses. In the interior there is a centre altar, and two side ones. And in front of the church a lofty pedestal surmounted by a cross.

The chancel roof is invariably higher than that of the nave. I know no people so teachable as the Syrian Christians, but they must be taught by those who can sympathize with them.

The Church Missionary Society once made an effort, by the establishment of a college at Cottayam, to lead them—with what effect, where so many prejudices existed on both sides, may be easily imagined.

The gathering in of the "Christians of St. Thomas" would indeed be a grand harvest. May God be pleased to give it to His Church!

In all my dealings with the native Christians of Southern India, nothing struck me so much as their delight in a seemly ritual. With that of Rome constantly before them, with the Eastern ritual of processions and grand displays, they are already acquainted; and they long for a ritual in their religious worship, which shall show forth to them " the beauty of holiness."

This will be the *key-note*, I am persuaded, of the conversion of thousands to the Catholic Faith; and it is, and has been, the key-note which has won for Rome her innumerable converts of the present day.

Yes! great and glorious would be such a harvest, already ripe for the gathering.

> " Work to be done; a Master to be served;
> Fields white for reaping; judgment hard at hand;
> O Lord! what thoughts are these! "

The Malabar Church possesses, as I have already stated, the three-fold ministry— bishop, priest, and deacon. They have always used for sacred purposes the Syrian tongue, a dialect of which was the language of Judea when our blessed Lord was upon earth. Bishops in regular succession under a metropolitan have ruled their Church, which at one time amounted to 16,000.

"A liturgy and other common prayers in Syriac mark their adherence to primitive antiquity.

"Their infants have been baptized from time immemorial; and whilst observing a considerable degree of ceremonial, they abhor the use of images in worship."

CHAPTER XIII.

The backwaters of Travancore—Quilon—Scenery—The boatmen—Travancore money—Method of counting —The museum—Appointment to curatorship—The gardens and menagerie—The lion-house—Curator's bungalow— Rabbit-warren—Deer park— Burmese way of catching deer—Tigers and their offspring— A tiger cat and his capture—A python fight—The aviary—The lakes—A half-shade garden—Nutmegs —Plantain and description—The ostrich—Owlery.

"Who created all things, is better than all things;
Who beautified all things, is more beautiful than all things;
Who made strength, is stronger than all things;
Who made great things, is greater than all things."

S. AUGUSTINE on Psalm xxxix.

I HAVE mentioned in a former chapter the out-station of Quilon, variously spelt Collam, Coulam, and Coilon. The name in Tamil signifies " a tank."

It was said to be built A.D. 825, and the

natives of Malabar begin their era at the period of its foundation, saying "so many years after the foundation of Collam."

The Portuguese had at one time a large fortress here, near *Tangancherry*, and there was once an independent Rajah of Tangan-cherry; but he was conquered in 1874 by a Rajah of Travancore and his territory annexed.

Government now keeps Sepoy troops here, according to treaty, for the protection of Travancore, and the chaplain is under orders to visit the station once a month.

The distance is forty miles, accomplished by water, sometimes in a canoe; but during the monsoon time, when the inland lakes are boisterous, in a "cabin" boat, manned with a dozen or more rowers.

There are on this journey, at several places, outlets to the ocean, the bars of which at times give way, and render the navigation very dangerous for smaller craft.

The "backwaters," as they are termed, are the great water-ways of the country, connecting the southern and northern districts, and running no less a distance than 200 miles in length.

Between Trevandrum and Quilon, however, there was a serious barrier in the form of a huge hill. The Government had constructed one tunnel, and since my departure have completed the second, by which means the waters are now continuous.

At the time I am writing of, the excavations were in progress, which gave the chaplain a small colony of Europeans to look after.

But to return to the "backwater" journey. Villages dot their sides here and there; and the traveller notices, as he passes along, the contrast afforded by the white Syrian and Romo-Syrian churches, standing boldly forth, with cross on summit, and affording a strong relief against the dark evergreen leaves of the Palmyra and cocoanut palms.

And who can describe the beauty of the vegetation! its lovely creepers! Take, for instance, the gloriosa superba, with its bright orange and yellow flowers so curiously and yet artistically arranged. "The flower, large as a lily, hangs down, and the petals, and stamens, and style all turn up, and grow up like a plum turned inside out; then, to complete the oddity," remarks Colonel Drury, "the leaves prolong their extremities into tendrils, and the plant walks on its toes."

Then view the pretty lantana, with its button-like form of varying colours of white and pink, and brown and yellow.

Or see again the cerbera, with its beautiful white flowers in clusters, or its pendulous fruit, so deadly to the taste.

Then, again, the pretty blue sarsaparilla. But it were an endless task to name them— all so beautifully placed in their banks of mangrove and fern.

At times, and especially by moonlight, as you glided along in your canoe, it was witnessing the most lovely tableaux imagination, aided by nature, could picture.

And then the eerie-ish scene presented to you: after traversing for some miles a narrow canal, all at once you shoot out into a broad expanse of shallow water, to find it studded with dark naked men, spearing fish by torchlight.

One generally travels by night, to avoid the great heat of the day; but very little sleep will you get if your rowers are lively and see a good prospect of "buksheesh."

They sing, and in such sharp, metallic tones, as Dryden sings,—

"A hundred mouths, a hundred tongues
  And throats of brass, inspired with iron lungs."

One man giving the refrain, and the others then taking it up.

In motion, too, far different to the delicious gliding of the Venetian gondola, and the only occasional cry of the gondolier, which soothes rather than disturbs you, as he turns the sharp corner of one of his watery streets.

The endurance of the boatmen surpasses all belief. Hour after hour they toil at the oar—and such an oar! a straight pole of bamboo, with an oval piece of wood tied to its extremity, and no feathering at all in the case.

And then the eager gaze of the poor fellows

as they crowd around you to see what "buksheesh" the sahib will give, the journey ended! How grateful they are for small mercies, to be sure! But then, again, how much they can get for their money!

The rupee—two shillings—it is presumed is divided into sixteen annas of $1\frac{1}{2}d$. each, or in Travancore currency, into twenty-eight and a half chuckrums—a small round piece of silver money, weighing six grains. That is divided again into sixteen cash (copper).

A single chuckrum is worth about six-sevenths of a penny. They are so small and globose that they are very easily lost; they are like silver seeds. It would take 28,500 chuckrums to make 100*l*. sterling.

Hours, therefore, would be wasted in counting them; and to prevent this calamity, they are counted by means of a "chuckrum board." This is a small, square, wooden plate, with holes, the exact size of the coin, drilled in regular rows on its surface. Each board contains from fifty to two hundred or more of these holes, which represents so many rupees.

A handful of coins is strewn over the board; then it is gently shaken, so that the coins fill the spaces, the rest being swept off with the hand, and then you see at a glance the amount you have. Each cash is said to purchase a certain amount of fruit, tobacco, vegetables, or other commodity which to the native is a necessary of life.

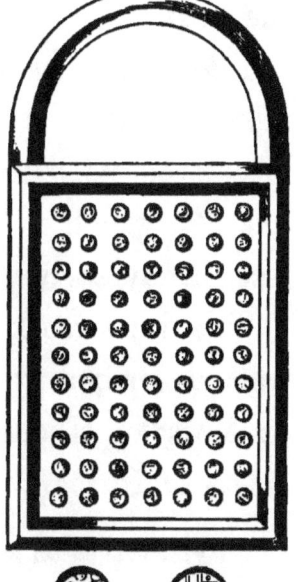

A great proportion of a chaplain's active duties are performed early in the morning and after sunset. In large stations, where there, are many hospitals, dispensaries, and schools to visit, these are all inspected by mid-day.

CHUCKRUM BOARD AND COINS.

The occasional duty in a small station like Trevandrum was very light, and left much time for other employments. I had not long been resident when the curatorship to his Highness the Maharajah's museum, and secretaryship to his Highness's public gardens, became vacant.

The British Resident recommended me to his Highness, and, with the consent of the British Government, I was allowed to accept the post.

I could not have selected an appointment more suited to my inclinations. It in no way interfered with my pastoral duties, and was one for which I had been trained, more or less, in my early years.

The day's work now allotted to me may be well described to the reader in the words of MAISTER HERESBACH, the author of "*Four Books of Husbandrie.*"

> " Fyrst served on knees the Majestie Divine ;
>   My servantes next and ground I overlooke,
> To every man his taske I doe assigne ;
>   When this is done I get me to my booke."

There was a small bungalow to reside in, well suited to a man living *en bachelor*, and an honorarium attached to the office. It had once been held by an eminent Indian botanist, Colonel Drury, who had done much to promote that science ; but hitherto the museum itself had been very much in the background.

It was a chaotic mass of curios; these different collections were added to, classified, and made a means of education to the masses. The Maharajah, however, took more pleasure in the gardens than in the museum; but the First Prince of Travancore, now the Maharajah, evinced a most intelligent appreciation of the museum's needs and opportunities; and, I have no doubt, will strengthen greatly the hands of his Highness's present curator.

Some short time before my arrival, the Travancore Government had laid the foundation-stone of a museum, to commemorate the Governorship of Lord Napier.

The design was made and carried out under the supervision of the accomplished Government Architect, Mr. Chisholm. It was designed after the Travancore style of architecture, which closely resembled the Phöngyee House style of Burmah, and was well fitted for the purposes for which it was intended.

The public gardens, in which the museum

T

was itself situated, covered a space of about fourteen or fifteen acres, and were picturesque in the extreme, consisting of plain, hill, and dale.

They were adorned with the most beautiful flowering-trees and shrubs, of every variety. The leisure hours of an Indian Padre are most frequently employed in his garden, as mine for some years had been: I had now to carry this out on the landscape footing.

For several years the gardens had been uncared for, since Colonel Drury's departure; and the menagerie—which most native princes delight in—left to take care of itself. The gardens had become a jungle, and the menagerie an unsavoury thing, and inhumane withal.

There was a very fair reference library attached to the museum, wherein I found Hughes' "Landscape Gardening," a book dealing with principles, which greatly assisted me in my work.

The London Mission Missionary I also found an accomplished botanist, and always willing to assist me in a difficulty.

The animals were scattered here and there, all over the gardens, with and without shade from the pitiless rays of the sun.

There was a large tiger's den, divided into different compartments, with tigers and lions. It was close and ill-ventilated. The plan was a good one—one central compartment and eight radiating ones.

A handsome lion-house was in course of construction. This I had rapidly finished, and housed my lions in splendour and comfort.

It consisted of a huge square building, with sloping Travancore roof, containing a large dormer-like opening on each side. There was a large den for the male and female lion, and some small cubs—a good tank leading out of this for bathing ; and two smaller dens. We had in all eight lions. In the larger den were two couches, made of black-wood, for their majesties, *père et mère*, to repose upon. And very grand they looked posing themselves unconsciously—a beautiful study for any artist. They were the ordinary Indian lion. When the progeny became too numerous—for they were very prolific—we exchanged them for different animals, with other native princes.

In this way we obtained a rhinoceros. I now altered the ventilation of the tiger's den, and built a verandah round it, supported by

GARDEN LODGE.

pillars of the Indian black-wood, handsomely carved.

But I must locate myself in my small bungalow. I had all my windows wire-netted outside, which enabled me to sleep with them open at night time, protecting me, in case of any of the animals getting loose, from an invasion of territory. No animal would attempt to enter anything so much like a trap, unless it heard within perchance the bleat of a goat or tethered victim.

I had a centre room, which served for sitting, dining, and library, a bed-room, and "preparation-room" for my specimens, bath-room, and a butler's pantry.

My cook-room of course was outside, at the back of the bungalow, in a grove of beautiful trees. I now had a band of masons and carpenters, sawyers and blacksmiths, hard at work, the Government giving me *carte blanche* to erect whatever I thought necessary.

I had plenty of gardeners, and two large gaols gave me extra aid for purposes of road-making, excavation, &c., in the form of convicts.

I laid out my bungalow garden, wherein was a tank with young crocodiles in it, and a mound of flowering cactus, with an incipient cobra family.

Near at hand was a rabbit-warren, and here experience taught me that rabbits and hares would live in harmony together. Not

far off was the deer park, an extensive plot
of ground, with some fine shelter-giving
trees. Here lived in tolerable harmony a
small herd of spotted deer (*axis*), some
sambhur, and an ibex caught in the hills.

We had also a pretty *muntjack*, though
not placed in the park, a most delicate, lady-
like little deer in miniature, with its peculiar
V-shaped mark on its forehead.

The Burmese have a peculiar way of
catching deer and killing them, which I will
mention here. They go out in a party,
selecting a dark night. A man walks in
front, having a large lantern with a powerful
bull's-eye, on his head. He carries a bell
in his hand, which he occasionally tinkles.
The deer approach the light, appear fasci-
nated by it, and are easily speared or cut
down with their dhà.

But let us go off to the tiger den. Those
we had were called the "Bengal Royal
Tiger," and a noble pair they were. Before
I became Curator, they had produced several
litters of cubs, which had invariably died.

One morning my head native superintendent informed me that the tigress had "children." *Three, of course,* that seems to be their usual number—a providential arrangement, doubtless, that they are not as prolific as other cats.

How were we to keep these alive?

I had the den matted-up, sufficiently high, as I supposed, to prevent the native visitors from seeing and disturbing the mother.

But, alas! in vain. Their curiosity is unbounded, and look they would, "exploring every place with curious eyes;" so the tigress sulked, and refused to rear her offspring, and they were too young to bring up by hand.

A few more months, and we had another litter. This time I gave up the centre compartment and an outer one to the tigress and her cubs. Here she could drag them away, like a cat carrying her kittens, into the dark, and nurse them undisturbed. Meantime, I fed her liberally with buffalo milk, in addition to her daily ration of meat.

I reared in this manner two out of the three cubs. The third cub, I was told

by an old shikari, or native hunter, who
had spent most of his life in the jungle,
always died; and with us it invariably did
on the ninth or tenth day, apparently from
fever.

MY NIMROD.

All the animals
were fed alter-
nately on beef
and goat. In the
tiger den we had
the former, some
cheetahs, and a
black panther pe-
culiar to Travan-
core. The spots
could only be seen
when in the full
sunlight.

We had also a
fine specimen of
a tiger cat (*Felis
Nepaulensis*), as large as a cheetah. I will
narrate how he was caught. My shikari, or
hunter, who occasionally brought me in wild
animals for the gardens, lived just below them.

He was disturbed one morning by the uneasiness of his dogs, and went to see what was the matter, when they finally turned out a splendid " tiger cat." They chased him to the banks of a tank, into which he was forced to betake himself.

The shikari ran to the other side of the water, sent off a coolie for a rope, and divested himself of his upper garments. He then, taking the rope in his hands, plunged in to meet his foe.

He met him, and succeeded in throwing a cloth over the animal's head, and with the assistance of the coolie noosed his fore-legs, and afterwards securing them all, brought his captive to the gardens.

For about three days the animal refused food altogether, though at night-time he quenched his thirst. In the end, nature asserted her dominion, and he ate, though only at night. In a fortnight he was tame enough to eat in the day-time, like his more civilized fellow animals.

We had a python cage, with a couple of python in it; another was added to the collection. At first they were friendly enough, or else too comatose to be belligerent.

One morning, on seeing the usual chickens put in, which was done every third day, a grand battle ensued. The two combatants coiled themselves round each other, and then with a sudden twist, which can only be described as quickly tying a knot with your own body round your adversary's, they gave a prolonged squeeze to each other, which seemed for the time to meet all requirements, though one died from its effects on the following day.

CHAPTER XIV.

"'Well, Master Notary,' quoth Sancho, 'there is a great deal to be said on this subject.'"—CERVANTES.

ALL the larger animals I had now rendered very comfortable, so my thoughts were turned to the birds.

For them I constructed a large aviary. It was a circular building, about fifty feet in diameter, with a shingled roof of red and white cedar. The sides were wire-netted between iron pillars. A tree was in the centre, with rockery work at its base, and an abundant supply of fresh water.

We had all kinds of pigeons at liberty, parrots, cockatoo, hornbill, and in some smaller compartments, quail, mynas, doves, landrail, &c. There were some beautiful jungle fowl with their exquisite plumage, Guinea-fowl, and Mexican duck. Also a compartment for the " hill" and " flying squirrel."

The hornbill was the most imitative of all the birds; it could catch the notes of any other bird, but preferred that of the Guinea-fowl, probably as being the most obtrusive. The male of this bird is said to plaster up his mate during the incubating season in a hole with mud, and to feed her attentively until the brood is ready to come forth.

In the lower part of the garden were a series of excavations, made for the purpose of obtaining brick-clay for the museum building.

This space occupied about a couple of acres of ground, where water was easily procurable. I set 200 convicts to work at this to remove the intervening masses of earth, and in about three months we made a very good lake, leaving here and there sufficient ground to form an island.

There was a fine broad walk on the banks, planted already with " Cerbera " and the *Pandanus,* or *Screw Pine* trees.

The Cerbera is a very beautiful tree, with its dark laurel-like leaves and its clusters of white flowers. Its fruit is in the shape of a mango and not unlike it, or a greatly magnified egg, say an emu's.

The seeds are poisonous, and as deadly to the taste as the bite of " Cerberus " was said to be of old. The *Pandanus* has long prickly leaves, set screw-wise, with a large pine-apple kind of fruit of the same colour and appearance. When cut open with an axe it is found to be composed of a tough, woody substance.

The natives affirm that crystals are to be found in them. It is quite uneatable I should think. Its roots obtrude themselves out of the banks, and give the tree the appearance, it has been remarked, of walking on stilts.

For the water-fowl, on one of the islands I built a Chinese pagoda. Sloping upwards from these lakes—for there were two—was a large space of ground, converted into a half-shade garden. It was already planted with fine trees, mango, vanilla, Palmyra, date palm, sago, coffee, nutmeg, Alexandrian laurel, and other beautiful flowering shrubs, together with the fine broad-leaved plantain.

The nutmeg-tree is well worthy of a few remarks, for which I am indebted to Mr. Porter:—"The fruit is smooth, externally pear-shaped, and about the size of a small peach. It consists of an outer fleshy covering, called the pericarp, which when mature separates into nearly equal longitudinal parts or valves; secondly, of the aril or mace, which when uncut is of a light-scarlet colour; and thirdly, of the seed proper, or nutmeg.

"This is enclosed in a shell, which is made of two coats, the outer hard and smooth; the inner thin, closely invests the seed, which, being coloured, impart the marbled or mottled appearance characteristic of the nutmeg. Good nutmegs are distinguished by being large, round, heavy, finely mottled, and of a light-grey colour."

I have no intention of describing all the trees we had in this prettily-shaded spot; but I must say a little about the plantain, with its golden bunches of fruit, weighing from twenty to ninety pounds.

In some countries it supplies the place of bread, and is highly nutritive. Indeed, it is said to yield as much as five pounds of meal from an average bunch weighing twenty-five pounds.

The leaves in a dried state are used for thatching; and the stem and leaves abound in fibre, useful for textile or cordage purposes, and forms an excellent material for the finest or the toughest kinds of paper.

The root of the plant is used medicinally, and its leaves as a cooling dressing for blisters; but care must be taken, as each side of the leaf possesses a different use.

It also yields a dye, often substituted for marking-ink.

But we must leave this shady retreat, with its ferns, caladiums, and grasses, and ascending a flight of steps, visit the ostrich enclosure. This is an oval building, light and airy, with sloping roof and beautifully carved teak cornice.

The enclosure itself is made by a wall, about three feet and a half in height, composed of boulder stones, with ferns growing in their interstices.

The top is formed of iron stanchions here and there, and telegraph wire.

The ostrich is one of the birds, in common with cuckoos, hornbills, and some kinds of parrots, which possess eyelashes.

There were some falcons, owls, and kestrels yet to be housed. I had in my store some fine ebony doorways, which had been designed for the museum windows, but were found too small when their glass fittings arrived from England. These I used, fitting in the lower part of them with slabs of white and grey marble, and the upper part with diamond-shaped wire netting.

The back wall was extremely thick, and made of blocks of granite. There were doors at the back of each division for cleaning out the cages; and the recessed wall afforded protection for the owls in the day-time from the glare of the sun. A zinc roof, and some wooden carved cornicing finished the structure.

Intermediately with these different structures, road-making, draining, and planting were constantly going on. Country people frequently were bringing in animals of different kinds; one day it would be a deer, or a cheetah; another, a cobra, or a monkey.

The monkey season had arrived, and a very minute specimen, with a very blue little face, made its appearance. There did not seem much prospect of its living; but the natives, apart from their religious worship of them, are very much attached to them.

The poor animal had been very forlorn and miserable for a few days, when, fortunately, another monkey, with a young one almost as big as herself, was brought to the gardens.

She immediately abandoned the big baby, and took charge of the small one. A few days after this occurrence, another female monkey was brought in, who took to the

U

discarded child, and so all parties were satisfied.

We were getting so many now, that it was necessary to give them a domicile. For this purpose we excavated out of the side of a hill two chambers for them, twenty-five feet in length by twelve feet in breadth.

The hill-side was composed chiefly of laterite ; and where there was only earth, laterite was inserted ; so, with a zinc roof, and iron bars in front, we constructed the dwellings, one for the common brown greyish monkey, and the other for the black wanderoos, or lion-monkey.

The latter is a fine black fellow, with white beard and long tail, tufted at the end. We never found that they bred when in captivity. Cuvier, though successful, never succeeded in preserving those born in captivity, beyond a few hours.

There was a pole with lateral branches for them in each cage, swings, &c., and some looking-glasses inserted in the side breeding cages, which seemed to give them much pleasure.

Some of the very small monkeys could come in and go out at pleasure; and though enjoying their liberty, never attempted to escape altogether. It was very amusing to see them climbing up the native visitors, searching in their girdles for any stores of hidden grain.

In speaking of the larger animals, I omitted to state that we had a bear. Poor Bruin! He lived in a deep pit, the sides of which were of laterite. There was a wooden railing surrounding the top of the pit. It was a dark, dirty den, and the poor animal lived in a miserable state, particularly during the monsoon time.

There was a fine sloping hill near the monkey-houses : there it was determined to build him a den. This was done by excavating a large semi-circular space; the sides were coated with bricks, and the frontage was of iron bars, running some sixty feet in height.

There were two retreats for him in this chamber, recessed in the semicircular side, and bricked, for he was very fond of using his claws. There was also a second large chamber, for him to retire to when his den was cleaned, with a trap-door, which drew up and down.

There were flights of steps running on either side of these two chambers, connecting a lower and upper terrace.

In the centre of the den was a pole for exercise, upon which he threw himself, with a grunt and a swing of the body, to reach the coveted piece of bread held forth for him at the extremity of a long bamboo.

At the time I am now writing about, the outer flight of steps had not been finished, and we had not had any rain for several months; the ground was parched and fissured, and we were longing for the clouds to gather and a sound of abundance of rain.

It came with a force known only in the tropics. It was Sunday, and I was sitting writing to my children, and the downpour had been continuous for some hours, when my butler ran in, in great trepidation, to tell me that the flood had broken in the bear-pit wall, and that the bear was coming out.

I hurried out to the scene of action, the pit being within a stone's-throw of my bungalow. It being Sunday, there was no one about, and I only had my servant and one garden attendant.

I found a portion of the wall fallen in, and the bear standing on the débris; but, fortunately, not at the top of it, which came within two feet of the hill sloping between the terraces.

I sent off the native for a loaf of bread, and tried by my voice to coax the bear down to his second den; but nothing would induce him to move.

We then got a bucket in which his food was usually lowered, and let that down into the second chamber. He essayed to go in for that, but unfortunately the native who had hold of the chain suspending the trap-door, let it go too soon, and the animal became suspicious and timid.

In the mean time many natives had assembled, and three or four of them were bold enough to stand with me in the gap of the fallen wall.

We had armed ourselves with the first thing to hand, some short bamboos. The bear after his retreat from the door went and sat sulkily in one of the first chamber recesses.

It was necessary that he should be got out of this and into the second den, as we could not repair the gap, but all inducements in the way of food failed to move him.

We then let down some matting to cover this recess, which made him furious, but stirred him out of the position.

He then commenced walking about on his hind-legs, growling to the utmost, and then charged, to our horror, right up the débris incline.

When within half a dozen feet of the top I gave him a pretty sharp salute on the head, which caused him to retreat; ere he had done that, however, all the natives who had stood by me fled, though only to a distance sufficiently near to see me scalped.

I cried out to them to come again and open the trap-door. I had sustained four charges, and the infuriated brute was coming up again.

A native, my Mussulman superintendent, now fortunately came to my rescue, and got up the door.

The bear charged again, and I met him with a blow on the snout, which broke my bamboo to within a couple of feet of my hands.

I now looked round to see what could be done in the event of the worst, and had made up my mind for a roll down the hill, hoping thus to get separated from my antagonist. All this passed through my mind in an instant, but the last blow had given the *coup de grâce;* he whirled round and made a rush for the second door, was in, and the door closed upon him.

There may be some truth in what Hudibras asserts after all :—

> " The bear he never can prevail
> To lion it, for want of tail."

There was a shout of triumph from the natives, and I retired, a good deal wearied out, drenched to the skin, for it had been raining in torrents all the time.

The joy of the poor fellows was unfeignedly

real at my escape, which they attributed to the fact of my being a Padre.

I had just time to dress and be off to service, with grateful heart to Him who had saved me from the paw of the bear.

I dreamt of bears for three weeks afterwards.

About this time I had finished making some fine terraces in front of the museum, and had planted an avenue of the Indian cork-tree leading to its principal entrance.

These trees were collected from different parts of the garden, and were of the same growth, having reached the height of between thirty and forty feet. I transplanted them in the rainy season, with only the loss of the leaves for a short time.

It is quite astonishing what may be accomplished in this way in India with ordinary care. I have moved trees, one particularly, a *Poniciana regia*, or the "gold mohur tree," with its beautiful scarlet and gold blossoms, which took 100 convicts and my gardeners, another fifteen men, to carry from one position to another.

Some of these flowering trees are beautiful

in the extreme. The *Lagerstrœmia* is one peculiarly beautiful, with its purply-red blossoms, which cover the tree in rose-like clusters. In most of the flowering trees, when in full bloom you see the flowers only, and scarcely any leaves.

They are very striking objects sometimes in the jungle, where you come upon one in full bloom in the midst of other trees, with their differing coloured leaves, such as the patulous teak, with its great leathern leaves, and the spare-leaved peeple-tree, with its treacherous roots. The cork-trees have a handsome dark leaf, with most delicate white flowers, and look very picturesque.

Towards the end of one dry season I noticed a cork-tree covered with a kind of spider's web, with its filaments reaching to the ground. On examining it, I discovered that all the leaves had been

DENUDED TREE.

eaten up by small black caterpillars, who,

having finished their repast, were then migrating to " pastures new," reaching the ground by means of the gossamer-like threads they had spun.

In removing fallen timber we found the elephant most useful. It is impossible to watch his actions without interest, or without attributing to him a power of sagacity, which it is questionable, on the whole, whether or not he deserves. General Fytche, in his book on Burmah, has a passage relating to their sagacity, which I am sure the reader will pardon my introducing.

He says : " It is most curious to observe the wonderful sagacity of the elephants at work in those timber-yards, and their aptitude in comprehending what is required of them.

" They drag the timber to the appointed place, and with their head, tusks, trunk, and feet, and stack it in any form desired.

" The old ones accustomed to the work are most particular about the timber being correctly laid, and push the logs with their head until it fits exactly in its place.

" An officer, in an official report I remember, in describing their sagacity stated his belief that they actually squinted along the logs, to see, in military parlance, if they were ' properly dressed.' "

General Fytche was an officer of acute observation, and doubtless believed thoroughly in the cleverness of the elephant, instances of which, with his great jungle experience, he must have witnessed.

And this reminds me of a tale of him, in my time, in Burmah amongst the natives, which reported him as an invincible " shikari," the terror of wild elephants, and particularly of one rogue elephant with a deformed foot, and who, it was said, always quitted the district and scene of his depredations when the gallant officer was known to enter it.

Mr. Sanderson, however, who is also an authority in such matters, questions any supereminent sagacity on the part of the elephant.

On reflection, perhaps it may occur to many that most of the clever movements one has witnessed on the part of the elephant have been when the mahout was upon his back. However, not to anticipate, let us hear what the latter gentleman himself has written on this head.

He says, " I have a young riding elephant at present, often my only shooting companion, which kneels, trumpets, hands up anything from the ground, raises her trunk to break a branch, or passes under one in silence, stops, tacks, and does other things at understood hints, as I sit on her pad; but no uninitiated looker-on would perceive that any intimation of what is required passes between us.

" The driver's knees are placed behind an elephant's ears as he sits on it, and it is by means of a push, pressure, and other motions that his wishes are communicated, as with the pressure of the leg with trained horses in a circus.

" I have never seen one show any aptitude in dealing, undirected, with an unforeseen emergency."

Be this as it may, Mr. Sanderson, however, goes on to mention a fact well worth record-ing with regard to their swimming capabilities, and relates a tale of sending a batch of them from Dacca to Barrackpoor, in which they had to cross the Ganges and several of its branches.

He says, " In the longest swim they were six hours without touching the bottom, and after a rest on a sandbank, they completed the swim in three more: not one was lost."

From elephants, however, we may proceed to elephants' tusks. The Travancoreans are peculiarly expert in carving ivory. I have frequently seen them with a piece of rough ivory in hand, carving with a rude piece of steel the model of one of my deer in the garden park.

Equally clever are they in the way in which they carve and manipulate the horn of the buffalo, out of which they make many things, from a walking-stick to the model of a lizard. The horn is softened and made pliable by being held over the fumes of a charcoal fire, and at the same time anointed with oil.

Much has been said and written with regard to the discovery of toughened glass. It has been in a rude manner known for ages in Travancore.

The natives wrap the article of glass in grass, put it in a chatty of oil, which is then placed on the fire, and after having been boiled is allowed to cool gradually. Glass thus heated will last for years with ordinary care.

A friend of mine had preserved his lamp chimney glasses for nine years in this manner. The principle of unbreakable or toughened glass is, I understand, the passing of the melted substance through oil. Of a truth, "there is nothing new under the sun."

We must now proceed with the garden work. On the north side of the museum there was a depression of about fifteen feet to meet the level of the lower terrace. This left a large surface-wall of earth to be dealt with, and a well seventy feet deep to be preserved.

To do the latter it was necessary to construct a tunnel thirty feet long. The face of this tunnel made the centre of the wall; and opposite to that I erected a handsome foun-

tain, which played every band evening, by
means of pipes I laid down, connected with
one of the museum towers, which stood
seventy feet higher than the terrace.

On either side of the tunnel opening I now
constructed a façade. It consisted of inter-

GARDEN FAÇADE.

lacing arches, the triangular interlacement
filled with white marble, and the large openings with some of Minton's most beautiful
tesselated tiles, interspersed with tiles of
white marble.

The arches were built in brick, and covered
over with chunam or plaster—that being

composed of marble-dust and lime. I secured the marble-dust when cutting into squares some broken slabs. I converted them into tiles to intersperse with Minton's.

The effect was extremely good, as one obtained all the soft toning marble gives as a structure.

The façade was completed at each end by large flights of broad steps about twenty feet in length, the sides of which were filled in with encaustic tiles.

The top of the façade was finished off with an elegant parapeting.

On either side of the fountain I erected a pavilion and a band-stand, the latter designed by the chief engineer, each of them leading to different terraces.

The pavilion was intended as a place of rest and shelter in the heat of the day. Its length was about fifty-five feet, and its breadth thirty.

It was floored with large slabs of Italian marble, and furnished with seats, and groups of flowers here and there.

In this structure I brought into use some

of the ebony window-frames which had been rejected from the museum.

The narrow ones served as windows, by being filled up to the height of two feet with encaustic tiles. The broader ones served for doors, with a handsome pillar on either side. Above the wall-plate of the building was some handsome Saracenic work, done in plaster in colours, with a Japanese roof, and a cornice of teak-wood handsomely carved.

I next had to design and construct a house for the self-applauding peacock, who

"Treads as if some solemn music near,
　His measured step was govern'd by his ear,
　And seems to say, 'Ye meaner fowl, give place ;
　I am all splendour, dignity, and grace.'"

This may best be described as a square building with four faces, and a square cut out of each corner.

There were four large dormer-shaped openings in the roof *à la Travancore*, which was tiled, and laid in bands of colour.

The openings, or faces, were filled with wire net-work, and it was lofty, as the

proud peacock loves to roost in high trees.
Our stock was the common peacock of the
jungle—that is, the garden one of England;
but we had the promise of some white
peacocks from Baroda.

Peacocks were frequently brought in by
the jungle people for sale, perched on a
bamboo, to which they steadily clung. Poor
birds ! the natives, to prevent them fluttering
or damaging their plumage, had sewn the
eye-lids together, or thrust the stem of a
feather through them, to prevent their
seeing.

A native has very little idea of what
cruelty means, and will leave animals in
torture for days rather than waste, as they
think, a bullet or a little time in putting the
object out of its misery.

Near this house was a fine ˙space of
ground, stored with well-grown trees. This
was converted into a fernery.

To accomplish these transformations
rapidly, required only a little forethought.
Carts sent out into the jungle for ferns, and
orchids, and other hidden beauties of Nature,

soon filled up a space of ground prepared beforehand by a band of convicts—and then an Aladdin garden had sprung up.

In preparing the ground several ant-hills had to be cleared away, which gave diligent work for the pickaxes, and filled a preparation bottle with the queen white ants.

The Travancore queen is not so large as the ordinary queen ant, and is striped with a dark-brown band.

I opened many of these ant pyramids when residing at Bangalore, with the object of obtaining the queen ant, and thus getting rid of a destructive community in my garden.

The pyramids or mounds seldom in India, as far as my experience goes, exceed more than between four and five feet in height.

In New Guinea, however, M. D'Albertis says that they were so lofty when seen on the crest of a hill as to be mistaken by him for native constructions. He measured several which were ten feet high and thirteen feet at the base. And Mr. Schweinfurth reports

them as being fifteen feet high in the
Soudan.

The mounds are composed of earth and
sand, strongly agglutinated by means of the
saliva or other juice of the insect. After a
little exposure they become so hardened as
to resist the force of the rains, for two or
three years at least.

After clearing away the top, and digging
for about a couple of feet, you come upon the
nest proper.

And what a busy scene it is, with its
innumerable crowd of minute insects of a
straw-like colour, all hastening on their
different errands through the magazines,
galleries, and cells of their city !

At last, in one particular position you
come upon the *elliptical cell* of the queen
ant, who lives by herself in solitary dignity.

She is a huge caterpillar, about two and a
half inches in length, and three quarters of an
inch in breadth.

As you place her in the palm of your hand,
what a curious object she is ! How wonderful ! you exclaim, as you observe her body

surging with wave-like motion, and exuding at every pore her minute offspring.

I preserved my specimens in spirit, with the exception of one, which my head-gardener begged me to give to an under-gardener, who was consumptive.

White-ant eating is considered a specific against the disease, and the devouring of a " queen " a certain cure. So I gave up her majesty; whereupon the head-gardener nipped off her head and tail, and the subordinate, throwing back his head, opened his mouth and displayed a throat.

QUEEN ANT.

Was it a throat? Certainly not. It appeared to me a gullet only, similar in character to a two-inch leaden pipe *sans uvula!*

Down the lad's throat was the insect dropped, whereupon he violently rubbed his chest, and ran up and down the drive, evidently, to *settle* the subject.

As the mosquito may be considered the
" water scavenger," to save us from all the
ills of impure water, so the white ant may be
regarded as the " earth scavenger," to save
us from pestilence.

They live chiefly on vegetable substances ;
and if your grass be left too long uncut,
though not partial to out-door work they
will devour it.

What they chiefly love most is a dark
corner, where they may undisturbedly feast
on paper, cotton cloth, leather, or old wood.

To avoid the light, and work without
interruption, they build little clay tunnels,
sufficiently large for them to traverse.

There are certain chemicals which, mixed
with the plaster forming your floors, keeps
them aloof. They dislike indigo ; and so it
is customary, where carpets are used, to line
them with an indigo-dyed cloth.

Floors for the most part in India are
covered with rattan, or other country matting. In the most cleanly kept house it is
impossible to keep away altogether these
little pests ; and the reason is, that their larvæ

are mixed up with the building materials, and so appear in very unexpected places.

One day's neglect of sweeping all clear may cause irreparable damage; consequently anything that is obliged to stand on the ground is put on castors of glass, metal, or stone.

They have, as Mr. Robinson amusingly writes, a "head office in most verandahs, with branch establishments in the bath-rooms, while their agents are ubiquitous."

The same writer gives a humorous description of them when, preparatory to death, they are shedding their wings.

" Ruthless, omnivorous, the white ant respects nothing. And when in the rains it invades the house, what horrors supervene! The lamps are seen through a yellow haze of fluttering things; the sideboard is strewn with shed wings; the night-lights sputter in a paste of corpses; and the corners of the rooms are alive with creeping, fluttering ants—less destructive, it is true, than in the ' infernal wriggle of maturity,' but more noisome, because more bulky and more obtrusive.

" The novelty of wings soon palls upon the white ant ; they find they are a snare, and try and get rid of them as soon as possible."

I may add from my experience another scene to the drama. Imagine, then, amidst all this confusion dire, the servants rushing about in all directions, with dishes containing water, and lights to attract the insects : soon are the dishes full, when they are borne off triumphantly, to make curry for Ramosammy's repast that night.

In Africa, many a European has been driven to make a similar repast, and enjoy it, as Mr. Schweinfurth, for example, did in the Soudan.

CHAPTER XV.

Black ants—Red ants and their peculiar nest—The resurrection plant—Importation of tiger cubs—Wild dog—Insectivora—Remarkable nests of the humming-bird—Tailor and weaver birds—Edible nest of the swallow—A Durbar—The late Maharajah of Travancore—The Durbar physician in Highland costume—Native expedients for clothing—Umbrella, a badge of freedom—Anecdote.

" Who hath adorned the heavens with stars ?
Who hath stored the air with fowl ?
The waters with fish,
The earth with plants and flowers ?
But what are all these, but a small
Spark of Divine beauty ? "

BONAVENTURE.

HAVING in the last chapter spoken of the white ant, a few remarks regarding the large black and red ants of India may not be considered out of place. The former frequently take possession of the nest of the white ant, when forsaken, or any entrance is to be found. They are to be seen in every direction, in the house and in the field; and the moment you open a white ant's nest they are in for the game, which they eagerly carry off.

As Mr. Robinson says,—"They are to be found marauding on every sideboard, and whose normal state seems to be one of 'criminal trespass.'

"See him bustling about, dashing about in all directions, continually losing his balance, scrambling out of dust-holes and crevices until he comes into collision with a blade of grass, which he utterly discomfits, and then on a sudden, tail up, he makes for home."

The red ant is a fiery-red little insect, constantly found on trees and bushes. Woe to you, if you find yourself treading in a nest of them in the undergrowth of the jungle, or by accident putting aside a branch of a tree with your unprotected hand !

They sting most vehemently, and make you desire beyond all things, like the swimming boys at Aden, to " Have a dive," to be free of them.

Du Chaillu speaks of them in South Africa, in a manner quite applicable to India.

He says: " This insect has a singular manner of building its nest. It prefers to live in certain trees, which, very often, are completely killed by those ingenious house-builders. They choose the end of a branch where there is generally a thick bunch of leaves. These leaves they glue together by their edges in such a way that they make a bag the size of an orange, and this is the nest. The bite of these ants is very painful, and their temper, as with most ants who can defend themselves, very vindictive."

I have now cleared my " Fernery " ground at the risk of tiring the patience of the reader. We have a good substratum of ferns and orchids from the jungle, to which we can add as opportunity serves. And this reminds me of a curious Mexican plant I found in the museum. It is the *Lycopodium lepidophyllum*, or " resurrection plant." It had been thrust aside amidst some odds and ends, looking quite old and dried up. I placed it in a globe of water, and in a few hours a green tinge came over it, its life revived, and in a few days it put forth new leaves. It had not been in water for *nine years*.

Every day some new plant, insect, or animal, was being brought to the gardens; and at this time I received three small tiger cubs. They had been found in a ryot's garden, in a tope of plantains, by his son, a young lad, who at first mistook them for cats. The father immediately placed scouts about, for fear of the tigress returning, and sent her cubs in to me.

They were not more than ten days old, one dying the following day, and one a month afterwards. I took every possible care of them; two men were detailed to sit up with them at night, and they were kept in my cook-room by the fire.

I nearly lost the third. One night one of the keepers came and woke me up.

" Sahib! Sahib!" "Well, who's there?"

"Please, Sahib, the child is very sick."

I went to inspect it—in dressing-gown and slippers—and administered some brandy with milk, had the animal well shampooed, and left it.

It recovered, and became a very fine tiger, and always recognized me, when placed in the larger den, by rubbing its nose against the bars of the cage, and purring at the same time.

We also had two puppies, brought in from the jungle, of the wild dog. These are very difficult to obtain, and have scarcely ever been known to live in captivity.

They were slim, and of a brown foxy colour, with forequarters slightly lower than the hind, and only lived two or three weeks.

It was the most extraordinary sight to see those dogs, I will not say eat, or devour, but *bolt* with incredible speed any portion of meat given to them.

In their wild state they burrow in the ground, and are the most indefatigable hunters of large game, which they pursue in troops, surround, and hunt in a circle, until the affrighted animal drops down from exhaustion.

I was constantly able to add to my collections, for the museum and my private one, as the natives discovered the things which pleased the sahib best.

I consequently soon made a fine insect collection. To enumerate the specimens would be too tedious and uninteresting perhaps to the general reader, but I will mention a few, by way of example illustrating the insectivora of the district.

The most common of all insects is perhaps the millepede (*Spirostreptus*), the ordinary

TRAVANCORE MILLEPEDE.

size of which is seven inches in length. It presents the appearance of a ring-armoured caterpillar, of a deep chocolate colour.

There is a stick insect (*Phasmidæ*) nine inches in length, looking exactly the colour of a piece of jointed bamboo, with six legs, the two foremost being six inches long, and the latter five, Flying lizards are not at all uncommon.

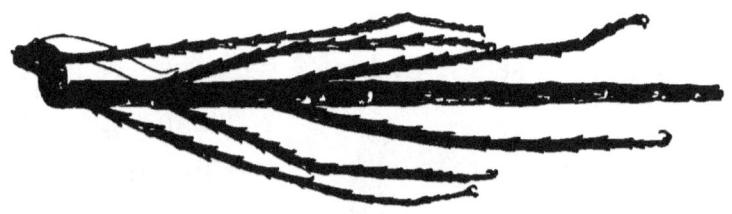

STICK INSECT.

The death's-head moth (*Acherantia atropos*) is very common in India, but not so large as in Europe. The specimens are well marked. I do not think any superstitious feeling is excited in the minds of the natives of India by their appearance, as is said to be the case in the British Isles amongst the illiterate.

The looking-glass moth (*Bombycidæ*) is more the size of a bird than a moth; the wings of my specimen measure from tip to tip nine and a half inches. It derives its name doubtless from four triangular marks of transparent talc-like texture in its wings.

I consider it remarkable also in the peculiar construction of its antennæ. They are three quarters of an inch in length and three eighths of an inch in breadth, presenting a red feathery appearance, as if the insect used them as a brush.

Possibly it may do so.[1]   It is a moth, and feeds on insects, which perhaps require

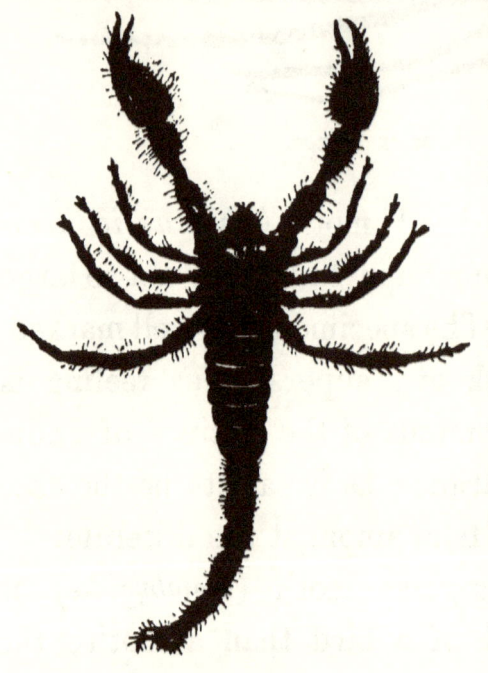

cleansing ere they are fit to be devoured. It reminds one of the goatsucker or nightjar, a bird with whiskers, which I have understood to be given for the purpose of brushing off the down of

SCORPION (half natural size).

the moths on which it feeds.

Scorpions abounded, of immense size, on

[1] Since writing the above, I am informed by Mrs. Hutchinson, the accomplished entomologist, that I am entirely wrong in my supposition, as the insect uses its antennæ as feelers, and in its perfect state is not supposed to feed at all.

the hills. I had some specimens four and a half inches in length from head to tail.

Stag-horn beetles, or rather those allied to them (*Odontolabis Burmeisteri*), as shown in the engraving, the elytra being of a gamboge colour divided by a line of black, also were very fine, measuring four inches in length and one inch and a half across the body.

Locusts there are of every hue and colour, some

ODONTOLABIS BURMEISTERI.

measuring three and a half inches in length. The damage done to the crops by an insect of such dimensions may be gathered from an extract from a Report of one of the Famine Commissioners of the Trichinopoly district which I here insert. He writes :—

" A great calamity has befallen a large tract of some fifty villages in the Perambore Taluk, a calamity greater than the famine.

The ravages of locusts we.·e something fearful; there was not a grain of cholum, umboo, or varaga left on the stalk. My road was crossed by swarms of these, and the road was actually covered by them one hundred yards before me. The young ones hop their march, while the winged ones lead the army.

" When they alight on fields the young ones stick to the root and eat the stalks down, while the bigger ones take their position on the ears and eat away the grain. You see a field after their devastation; the sight is most melancholy, as if a row of sticks were stuck in the ground; no blade, no ears, and no freshness in the plants, as if their vitality had departed from them.

"One ryot determining to cut his crop, green as it was, to save at least some of it, had collected labourers to do so the next morning; but to his amazement the whole had been eaten up during the night, and the locusts stuck to him in such numbers as threatened to eat him up alive."

And last of all, amongst the *Theraphosidœ* the bird-killing spider should be named, those

" Honest creatures who openly confess that they live on flies."

He has ten legs, a circular body two inches in length, and a proboscis of horn—a most formidable enemy to the little wee Indian birds, many not longer than an inch, though

TRAVANCORE SPIDER.

there is no case yet recorded in India of its bird-killing propensities.

My other collections consisted of bird and snake eggs, not omitting crocodiles, and a very valuable selection of shells collected at Ceylon. I must not, however, omit to mention the extreme beauty of some of the birds' nests

I collected. Notably two or three stand out conspicuously for remark.

We will begin with the largest of three, first of all. It is the weaver-bird's nest. It is composed of fine interwoven grass, oval in shape, about eight inches in breadth, narrowing into a channel entrance eighteen inches in length and about three in breadth. The length of the whole nest is thirty-three inches. They present a curious sight when seen hanging from the Palmyra-trees in great numbers.

The following description, by Mrs. Guthrie, is illustrated in the two accompanying engravings. This lady writes :—" The nests are very curious ; their shape has been likened to that of a retort.

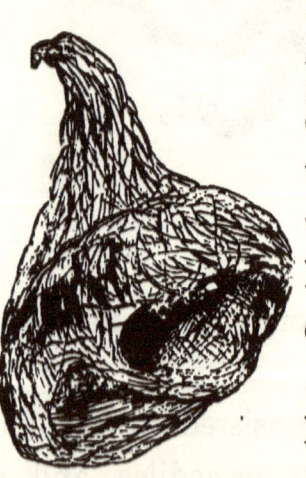

SECTION OF WEAVER-BIRD'S NEST.

" A pair begin their labours by forming a loop, in which when complete the female sits, leaving the male bird to fetch the materials and work on the outside of the nest, while she works on the inside, drawing in the fibres pushed through by the male, placing them in their proper position and smoothing all carefully.

" Patches of mud are found in some nests, which it is considered are meant to ballast them."

The first illustration shows a section of the nest, from one in my possession, and the second an entire nest.

The plumage of the bird is said to be a dull-brown, shaded with lighter tints of the same hue, and a tinge of yellow bordering.

Let us have a peep now at the Indian sun, or humming bird's. I will select one, built in my Indian verandah, on a rose-bush. It is in length five inches, composed either of the most delicate

WEAVER-BIRD'S NEST.

fibres of the Palmyra-tree leaf or of the bamboo, interwoven.

The interior of the nest is padded with silk cotton from the cotton-tree (*Bombax*); all over it, in patches, are silvery shreds of the silvery inner bark of the bamboo. A small circular opening of about three quarters of an inch in

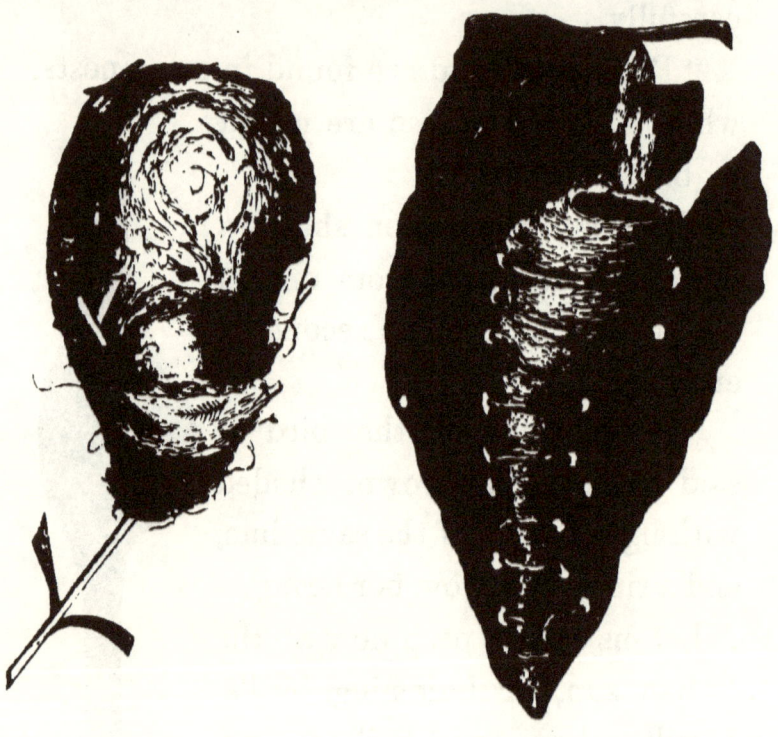

SUN-BIRD'S NEST.   TAILOR-BIRD'S NEST.

diameter admits the tiny inhabitant, and over this aperture is a little cowl, which, when it rains, by its own weight shuts up the nest.

Another interesting nest I shall attempt to describe is that of the tailor-bird. Its length is dependent on the leaf of the jack-tree. The bird selects a leaf, curls it round to make a funnel, stuffs it with cotton from the cotton-tree pod, and then sews the edges of the leaf together, leaving the knots made to secure them very distinct, and of a much larger character than an English seamstress would care to mark her work with.

The interior of the nest is warmly padded with silk cotton, and perchance the keen eye may perceive three lovely little eggs, about half an inch in length, pure white, with chocolate-coloured markings.

The nest is sometimes formed out of one leaf; but I have also seen two, and even three leaves, sewn together to make a habitation.

The bird is described as smaller than an English sparrow; its plumage light-brown with a mixture of olive green, and the tail has a narrow white border.

Beau Brummell's poem says,—

"The tailor-bird offer'd to make up new clothes
For all the young birdlings who wish'd to be beaus."

In some parts of Travancore the edible nest of the swallow (*Colocasia unicolor*) is to be found. Mr. Bourdillon visited some caves where he found the birds, nests, and eggs in a large colony of 200 or more. They exhibited no fear at his approach, and indeed were quite tame.

The nests were fastened to the rock with some gummy substance, almost transparent, and were composed of moss agglutinated with the same saliva. In form they were semicircular, and about two inches and a half in diameter. The eggs, pure white and longitudinal, looked like very pretty good-sized sugar-plums, being seven-eighths of an inch in length, and an inch in breadth at the widest part.

I procured some fine specimens of the eggs of the heron (*Ardea cinerea*); they are a pale-blue, the size of an English chicken's egg. There were many very curious eggs to be found, such as the vulture's, the giant crane, the bustard, the kite, Maraboo stork, with others too numerous to mention.

It was easy to obtain iguana's eggs; and I was fortunate enough once to get some of the cobra da capello and of the crocodile. These last are esteemed a great delicacy by the natives, and are eagerly sought after. They are very peculiar-looking eggs, being nearly four inches in length and two inches in breadth, of a white, glazed, porcelain-like appearance.

But we must pass away from these interesting objects, and attend a " Durbar," to which his Highness the Maharajah has invited the Reverend Chaplain and his European brethren resident in the station.

The durbar is a native levee, and usually held on some state occasion, such as the reception of a British Resident, or any change in that kind of ministry, when the Empress-Queen's letter is presented.

The gathering commonly takes place about sunset, when the Maharajah goes in state. In all Native States tributary to the British power there is in every station a "durbar hall," or place of assembly for such gatherings as that to which we are now going.

That at Trevandrum was the central hall
of the public buildings, which, with the
exception of the hall itself, was an ill-built,
ungainly mass of brick and plaster, used for
Treasury and offices.

The site, however, was a grand one, and
on the present occasion was thronged with
troops and band drawn up to receive the
Maharajah, and in the background a line of
elephants elegantly caparisoned; in fact,
all the imposing paraphernalia of peaceful
war.

Punctual to a moment his Highness arrives,
in an open barouche. The coachman drives
standing, and dressed in turban, scarlet coat
and trousers, as it is improper to sit in the
presence of royalty.

There are horse-keepers at the head of
each horse, and a crew of peons and half-
dressed natives, who all seem to be hanging
on in some mysterious manner behind.   :

" Admitted to the sight, would you not laugh ?"

" God save the Queen " is being played,
and the Rajah has walked up the hall through

a deep file of Europeans, backed by natives, and takes his place on the musjid or throne, with his Prime Minister at his side.

The royal anthem is again heard on the arrival of her Majesty's Representative, who is received at a stated distance by his Highness the Maharajah, and handed to his seat on the right side of the throne, though below it. Next to the Resident come different European officers, such as the Judge, Chaplain, Commanding Officer of the station, &c., and opposite to them the Royal Princes, and other Europeans of differing ranks.

The ceremony is opened by the Resident reading his commission or his message.

On this occasion it was the presentation of a banner and some title of honour. The Rajah had some years before received from the British Government the title of Maharajah for his loyalty to the English rule.

Then follows the reply read by the Dewan. This completes the business part of the meeting, and now follows the ceremonial.

The Maharajah receives from the hands of the First Prince a garland of flowers, which he places over the neck of the Resident, occasionally supplemented with flower bracelets. A small packet of betel-nut and chunam wrapped up neatly in tinsel, and some atta of roses presented to you on some wool, fastened to the end of a stick wound with red silk and tinsel.

The Princes then do the like office to all the Europeans present. The ceremony is then over; " God save the Queen" strikes up, and Maharajah, Resident, and garlanded guests depart, generally to meet at a state dinner afterwards, at which his Highness and the Princes attend, but eat not.

Speeches are made, and much pleasant intercourse during the evening ensues, enlivened with the strains of music proceeding from the band of his Highness's brigade. Fireworks often conclude the evening, in the manufacture of which the natives greatly excel.

I may here say a few words of

His Highness
Sree Patmanabha,
Dausa Vunchee Banla,
Ramah Vurmah,
Koolasekhara Rireetapati,
Munnay Sultan,
Maharaj Rajah,
Ramarajah Bahadur,
Shamsheer Jung,
Knight Grand Commander
Of the Most Exalted Order of the
Star of India,
Maha Rajah of Travancore.

His Highness was a man of small stature
and make, about forty-eight years of age,
with very small hands and feet, and of a pale
but intelligent countenance; his ancestry
dating back to *A*.D. 600. Nothing could
exceed his urbanity of manner, full of life
and vivacity, and naturally of a kind and
gentle disposition. He spoke English fluently,
and had established an excellent High School
in Trevandrum, which was doing an admirable English vernacular work.

"It is very difficult to say," remarks Bishop Milman, "what will be the result of an education which bears with it no shadow of religious teaching. The professors certainly were able and conscientious men, doing their secular work honestly and well; but I very much doubt if they will be able, as Dr. Duff says, by their system 'to create a conscience.' The result of such an education must be left then in the hands of Him, who alone can turn an imperfect system to His own glory."

His Highness was, I believe, much liked by European and native. I received the greatest kindness and courtesy at his hands; he was a *thorough gentleman*, with an instinctive appreciation of that qualification in others.

At all times he was accessible to his people, and listened with patience to their petitions. He was accustomed to receive his European visitors early in the morning at one of his bungalows in the cantonment, as he resided in his palace in the native portion of Trevandrum.

I call to mind one interview which is suffi-

ciently amusing to narrate. I, in company
with a very dear friend of mine, went to pay
our respects. At that time there was much
excitement in the station, for a very small
incident served to ruffle the waters in so
small a community.

The durbar physician of that time, an
eccentric but clever man, and a "loyal Scot,"
had just returned from furlough from his
native Highlands, and nothing would serve
him but to reappear on the Indian scene in
Highland kilt.

The natives had never seen such a stalwart
apparition before, and the European element
greatly enjoyed the freak.

.The appearance of the clever physician
was the "talk of the town," and soon after
the usual courtesies had passed we asked his
Highness what he thought of the costume.
The reply was that he thought it a *very grand
dress*, and had been given to understand that
it was as expensive as grand. But, added
the Maharajah, stuttering rather more than
usual, and running his hands over his knees,
" *I scare-are-are-cely think it is dē-ēcent.*"

Considering the scarcity of garments in which the native population indulge, the remark was sufficiently amusing.

There is evidently a good deal in colour; the dark skin attracts little attention, serving

A TRAVANCORE LADY'S PETTICOAT.
" Fashion, sole arbitress of dress."—Hor.

as clothing; whilst the white is, to say the least, somewhat startling.

It is only of late years, and through pressure from the British Government, that an order has been issued allowing the lower-caste people to cover themselves decently when in public.

They were considered in the eyes of the sacred Brahmin too low in the scale of humanity to require clothing, so that too much of the human form divine was displayed by these " country cousins " airing themselves in " town."

In the jungles of Travancore all restraint of that kind is set at naught, and both sexes may be seen with as little as that worn by our first parents: a few leaves suffice for the men, and an apron of grass of the most scanty proportions for the women.

Another proceeding on the part of the Travancoreans is one which arrests attention. Every other native you meet uses an umbrella, made very much on the model of those used by the Chinese, only covered with cadjan.

Now is the skull of the Travancorean less thick than that of his neighbour; and is he more sensitive to the rays of the sun ?

Not at all ; but in the days of *slavery* the common people were not allowed to use this emblem of dignity, and so now freely indulge

z

themselves in this mark of "liberty, equality, and fraternity."

The lower-caste people, whatever may be said of their taste in dress, have a very peculiar one for viands of rare descriptions. In pulling down an old building to make room for a better, my workpeople caught four dozen very fine rats, which the gardeners immediately took possession of *to eat.* They are very fond of "rats and mice, and such small deer," as also of the flying fox (*Pteropus Edwardsii*), one of the most unsavoury of batlike birds ; but then they possess a recipe for cooking it, from their own Soyer, which renders it a delicious morsel they aver, which may possibly be true, as they live on fruit only, for which they fly very long distances.

We all know how sad the strait was in the last siege of Paris, and how rats were at a premium, after all fancy dogs had long gone to their rest in dog-land. One day, I am told, a lady, driven to the last extremity by hunger, had her pet Fidèle dressed for dinner Much as she loved the dog, none the less did she enjoy her repast, and, re-grettingly viewing the remains, is said to have murmured, " *Alas! poor Fidèle!* HOW YOU WOULD HAVE ENJOYED THESE BONES ! "

CHAPTER XVI.

An architectural reverse—The pluviometer—Beetle catching—Insect ingenuity—Peculiar sands at Cape
Comorin—Farewell to native friends—A noble
Dewan—Adieu to India—The voyage—Perils of
the deep—A happy meeting—Work at home—A
poor wandering woman—Burial in woollen—Evan-
gelization—Finis.

" The world, oh brother, remains to nobody :
    Let us, therefore, bow our heart in God,
    And it is enough."
                                    SAADI, the Poet.

UP to this time I had been very successful
with my architectural designs and in completing their construction. I was now fated
to suffer a reverse—as the Prime Minister, the
Hon. Sashia Sastri, laughingly said, lest they
should get too proud of my services.

In the fort there were reported to be eight
fine stone pillars which the Sircar (native

government) were anxious to get rid of. They were accordingly sent to the gardens, with the hope of being made use of. We

ENTRANCE GATE.

were in want of a good entrance gate for the north side of the gardens, and so I worked them into a Saracenic design for this purpose.

All designs were submitted to his Highness the Maharajah for approval or to his Highness's Dewan (that is, Prime Minister). His Highness the Maharajah, however, took a particular fancy to the design, and requested me to erect it at the entrance of one of his H.'s bungalows in near proximity to the gardens.

The sides of the gateway were built up and the arch thrown, when we were overtaken by a most violent monsoon. For weeks the rain came down in torrents. We protected the work as well as we could, but in the end ineffectually.

Houses and walls were falling in every direction throughout the cantonment, and the material given me for construction was of such inferior make as to render the hope of successfully completing the building almost hopeless.

It was a band evening. My building superintendent had reported that the arch props could with perfect safety be removed, and so I had given permission for this to be done.

The band was playing, and I was sitting

in my verandah conversing with the Dewan, when presently an awful crash was heard. The Dewan started up and said, "*Surely a wing of the museum has fallen in!*" My heart sank within me. My pet project I knew had failed. The arch props had been removed, and a slight crack observed. The crack became a fissure, and gallons of water began pouring out of it, and then it fell in with a crash.

"*No, Mr. Dewan, the museum is safe. It is only my archway that has fallen. Let us go and see the ruins.*"

For a few moments I viewed them complacently enough, until my very dear friend the Judge came up, and patting me on the back, said, "*Dear old padre, we are all so sorry for you.*" I went back to my bungalow, but I didn't eat much dinner that night.

The following day I had bands of workpeople removing all traces of the building, as his Highness would never consent to drive under an archway which had once been known to give way.

The monsoon, so destructive to my pet archway, was still in full vigour, which reminds me of the care taken by the medical officers in registering the rainfall each wet season.

At Kamptee the infantry and artillery barracks are not more than one mile apart. The medical officer was greatly puzzled therefore at the difference in the fall registered at the different hospitals, until by accident it was found out that the Sepoy on guard at the artillery hospital, seeing the doctor a good deal excited at a heavy rainfall, made it still heavier on the first occasion he was on duty by pouring a half-pint of water into the pluviometer.

I was now busily engaged cataloguing the museum library, and drawing up a horticultural calendar giving directions to the native population when to sow and gather their fruits. In this I was greatly aided by Mr. Bain, the intelligent superintendent of his Highness's printing-press.

A great variety of insects also were brought in, and I was delighted one day with a very fine spotted beetle (*Hemiptera*), black, with gamboge-coloured spots. I asked my butler where he found him, but could get no reply, only "*Can't tell, master,*" and a broad grin. At last I said,—

" Well, Christopher Columbus, if you will not tell me, we shall have a row."

" Well, Sahib, I found him in the MALI's HEAD."

The insect was caught in the gardener's hair. Any further search was impossible. The gardener was a Naïr, and wore his hair tied up in a knot at the side of his head, and disdained a turban altogether. I found the arrowroot plant very favourable for catching the *Mantis*, the *Odontolabis Burmeisteri*, and the *Walking-stick insects* (*Phasmidæ*).

On stick insects Mr. Arnold has a very interesting passage.

" On a single occasion," he writes, " I obtained six varieties of *Bacteria trophinus* of most wonderful forms and shapes, some so like dried twigs that it was impossible at first to recognize them, and others accurately resembling fresh green leaves. Their appearance seems to protect them from their foes amongst the birds, and to enable them to obtain their food by surprise.

" Indeed, one of the most noticeable points in the insect world of the jungle was the way in which each small creature was protected by nature from its foes in some ingenious manner.

" Thus, when I have been searching under the bark of dead trees, it has been very observable that all the beetles harbouring there, and most of the other insects, have let themselves fall immediately they have felt the disturbance, and have become lost amongst the long herbage below. The success of this ruse when they are attacked by their chief foe, the woodpecker, is obvious."

There is no part of India which presents so favourable a field to the entomologist as Travancore. It would be endless to enumerate the stores obtainable from such a treasury of nature. From Cape Comorin to its most northern district it is full of wonders, entomological, botanical, and geological.

Amongst my different acquisitions I became possessed of specimens of three very peculiar species of sand, to be found at Cape Comorin in addition to the ordinary seashore sand. , The first closely resembled rice, and was, I believe, only disintegrated granite pounded very small by the action of water. The second was a very pretty red garnet sand, and the third a sand of a shiny black colour, possibly pulverized coal. The two latter were freely used by goldsmiths, and I found them invaluable for cleansing in my electro-plating pursuits.

The time was now rapidly approaching for me to take my last furlough and retire from the service, and bid adieu to this foreign clime and my European parishioners and native friends. And I did so with mingled feelings of gratitude and regret. The climate had dealt leniently with my constitution. During a residence of twenty years I had suffered only twice from dysentery, and once for a few days only from fever.

" When in this vale of tears I backward look,
And miss such numbers—numbers too of such,

Firmer in health and greener in their age,
And stricter on their guard, and fitter far
To play life's subtle game—I scarce believe
I still survive."

And with regard to my native friends, I can fully endorse what Sir Richard Temple has expressed in the following words : "The native character, as a whole, may be disparaged by some whose experience is short, and whose knowledge is not profound. But with an Englishman who lives and labours in the country, the wider his acquaintance with the natives, and the deeper his insight, the greater is his liking for them. He who has the best and longest acquaintance with the natives esteems them the most.

"Probably every Englishman who has during a lengthened residence been brought much into contact with the natives, parts from them with sincere regret, remembers them with the most kindly regards, and breathes heartfelt aspirations for their welfare and happiness."

I have frequently heard the natives accused of ingratitude, but I think very groundlessly.

I myself have received innumerable marks of love and gratitude from them. As regards the lower classes, they are outwardly moulded to whatever you wish them to become. They are as easily encouraged as discouraged.

If . treated like children with *love* and *firmness*, they will be found faithful unto death. Anyhow they will show affection to you which cannot be surpassed.

It was in one of the weary watches of the night, shortly after I had lost my dear wife, that the following scene occurred. I was sleeping, or rather trying to sleep, in a room next to that of my children. The Ayahs were sleeping on mats in the same room with them,—that adjoining mine, the half-doors being open.

When, as the hours went on, I found the head Ayah at my side.

"MASTER," she said, "*don't cry! I will take care of the children, and I will go across the sea with you, and when they have found another Ayah I will come back to my grandchildren.*"

And so she did, in spite of her dread of the " dark water ;" and when I left her at Southampton on board the steamer, her last words to me were, midst many tears, " *Mind you take care of* THOSE *children.*"

She had been in our service for fifteen years, had seen four of my children placed in " God's Acre," and had brought home with loving care the remainder.

She was a Roman Catholic; and God grant that when that day arrives when I shall be called to give up " my flock" we may all meet together around " THE THRONE."

I had received numberless courtesies from all the members of the royal family of Travancore, and much pleasure of an intellectual character from intercourse with the present Maharajah, then First Prince of Travancore.

But of all my native friends, none so thoroughly attached himself to my affections as the able and incorruptible prime minister, the Hon. Sashia Sastri, C.S.I. Previous to my departure his time of office had expired, and he had retired to his native village in the hopes of enjoying an honourable retirement from the cares of state affairs.

"An honest man's the noblest work of God."

says the immortal bard.

The British Government knew his value, placed him on their "Council," and finally settled him in harness again as Dewan of PUDAKOTTAI.

There would have been no evils of administration to redress had his presence not been required. He found an Augæan-stable work to perform, and zealously set about it. I shall only refer to one kind of reform which it has been his object to effect, and I shall state it in the words of his own report to Government.

The prevailing revenue system was the "*Amani.*" A very large portion of the lands under cultivation, and believed to be of the best kind, were held under this system. The property in these lands vested in the Cirkar (i.e. native government). He writes: "The ryots were in most cases tenants-at-will, and theoretically could be turned out without their consent. The transfer or sale of such lands was void at law. The crop raised by the ryot (at his own expense generally, and at times assisted with seed-grain from the Cirkar) was shared half and half between him and the Cirkar.

" To one who knows no more they appear to be just. What could be more fair?

" By sharing the crop equally, they equally shared the vicissitudes of season and market.

" During a life-long career of service I have had opportunities of watching closely the working of the Amani, or sharing system, in all its varied forms, in many districts of the Madras Presidency, as well as in Trancore, and my experiences have been of an interestingly sad character.

" It is a system saturated with evils and frauds of a grave nature. I will state briefly what is the case in the state of PUDAKOTTAI.

" (a.) The ryots, having no heritable or transferable property, have never cared to cultivate the Amani lands in due season. If you saw a bit of cultivation at the tail end of the season, the chances are it is Amani. Ryots prefer infinitely to cultivate other lands held in different tenures, such as Inam, Jeevitham, and many assessed lands. To prevent this, a penal agreement is forced from them to the effect that they would not fail to cultivate the 'Amani' lands first.

"(*b.*) As soon as the ears of the grain make their appearance, an army of watchers, called Kunganis (literally, eye-watchers) is let loose. As they get no pay for their duty, and are for the most part the old militia of the country, on whom this kind of work is imposed since fighting times had departed, and get a grain fee on the crop they watch, their watch is at best often lax.

"(*c.*) When the crop arrives towards maturity, it is the turn of Cirkar village officers, and the village headmen (called Mirasidars here) to go round the fields, and note down estimates of the crop. That there is considerable wooing and feeing at this stage goes for the saying. As in other matters, so in this, the race is to the rich and woe to the poor.

"(*d.*) As soon as the village officers have done, and reported the first estimate, down come special estimators from the Taluq Cutcheries to check the first estimate. Their demands have equally to be satisfied. Then comes the business of obtaining permission to cut and stack the crops. Here again another stage, where much feeing and grudge-paying takes place. If permission is delayed just two days, an adverse shower of rain irreparably damages the crop on the field, or over-exposure to the sun renders the grain unmarketable.

"(*e.*) Then comes the threshing and division of the grain on the threshing-floor. What takes place then may be imagined. If the outturn is less than the estimate, the ryot is made responsible for the *difference* without any further ado. If it is more, woe be to the *estimators*. The result in the latter case is often that the difference is made away with, and shared half and half between the ryot and officers concerned. During all this time, the unpaid army of watchers continues on duty.

" (*f.*) Now the Cirkar grain is removed to the granaries. Is all danger over now? By no means. A fresh series of frauds commences. The granaries have neither impregnable walls, nor are their locks Chubb's patents. The half-famished Vettiyan, the hereditary watchman of the village, mounts guard, and he and the village headman are personally held responsible for any deficiency which may occur on the re-measurement of the grain *out* of the granary. It often happens the poor Vettiyan, stung by hunger, is driven to certain deeds much against his conscience. Scaling over the mud walls, or forcing open the too easily yielding village locks, he helps himself from time to time to what his urgent wants may dictate. It is not often he is able to replace, even if he was so minded, what he has appropriated, before the day of reckoning comes. This comes sometimes soon, and sometimes late, depending on the time when the paddy is required for Cirkar purpose, or for sale to purchasers. When it does come, there is crimination and re-crimination without end. The Vettiyan charging the Mirasidar, and the Mirasidar the Vettiyan. The Cirkar officials, to vindicate its robbed rights, come down heavily on both, and often both are ruined. If the misappropriation is made in very small quantities, the way of replacement is very ingenious, a quantity of chaff, or a quantity of loose earth, or a quantity of big grained sand, is put in to make up the measure.

" (*g.*) Time passes and the months denoting favourable markets come round. There now remains the business of disposing of the Cirkar grain from the granaries. Simple as it may appear, enormous difficulty is experienced, and we have to face another series of frauds, now on the part of the Taluq or superior officers. Tenders are invited, but only a few come, and bid low. Tenders are again invited, but to no better purpose. At last come upon the scene a set of unscrupulous fraudulent tradesmen, or relatives or friends of those in authority, or mere speculators, professing to give security, which is really worthless. These men bid higher prices, and take up the grain in lots they require. They remove the grain, but make no payment down, but enter into promises to pay value in eight instalments, and profess to give due security for the fulfilment of the promise. It not unfrequently happens that the purchaser decamps, and his surety is found to have followed suit, or found to be hollow. The money due on the sales to the relatives and friends of the officers outstands the longest. If, to avoid these troubles, the grain is taken direct to the nearest market, to be there sold outright for cash, few could be induced to pay the market-price, the Cirkar grain being notoriously bad crop, and unscrupulously adulterated."

Such are some of the difficulties a revenue officer has to encounter in India.

To obviate all these evils the Dewan substituted a money assessment, which has proved a great success, put an end to an infinity of fraud, and simplified the public accounts.

A sad farewell to all my native subordinates, and I find myself at the hospitable table of my dear friend Major McNeill, with the transit at the door.

Strange moments these, in the bustle of departure, when the expectation of years seems on the eve of fulfilment! Expectations to be fulfilled now, in my case, in solitariness. Surely there must still be work to be done—and the children were at home.

> " Lead, kindly Light! amid the encircling gloom,
>   Lead Thou me on !
>   The night is dark, and I am far from home—
>   Lead Thou me on !

Kindly thoughts arise towards those with whom we have been companying. Irritations, if there have been any, vanish like the mist on the distant hills ; and acts only of love break upon the memory, as we part from those who have showed us " no little kindness."

A breathless messenger from the kind Maharajah comes just in time to find me, with a Governmental letter of thanks for my services; and a private note, enclosing a diamond ring as a souvenir of times that have bound us together.

Between Trevandrum and Colachel the forty miles are soon passed over, with fresh relays of bullocks, but not without the usual occurrence of finding oneself, transit and all, in a ditch, with the bullocks meekly submitting, with their patient eyes, to the catastrophe.

Colachel and fresh hospitality is awaiting me at the bungalow of good Mr. Grant, who alas! has now gone to the "far-off land," already peopled with his kindred and acquaintance.

A steamer in a few days arrived, and we embarked for Colombo, to meet the steamship *Almora*, which was destined to take us home to the "tight little island."

We had a fair complement of passengers—some of my late parishioners, which was very agreeable—as pleasant a captain and set of officers as one could possibly desire, and an excellent commissariat.

The passage was a very good one indeed until the last, when we came in for very rough weather, the conclusion of that storm in which the unfortunate *Eurydice* foundered, with all hands on board, and the news of which we learnt off Dungeness.

Many indeed are the perils of the deep; and amongst them is one, I should think, peculiar to the nineteenth century. On one occasion we were very nearly on the point of running down a collier. I was standing by the captain at the time, and remarked on its action in steering seemingly *in our way.* The captain laughingly said : *Ah, it will not do this time. The cargo is insured, vessel and all, and they are quite prepared for the emergency.*

Many a narrow escape we had, but at last found ourselves moored safely in the Victoria Docks.

Strange, and not altogether an unsatisfactory feeling was it, to find oneself bowling along in a hansom, instead of walking or driving amongst a crowd of semiclothed Travancoreans.

The following day took me to the neighbourhood of Oxford, where my children were
awaiting me. The baby boy was a baby no
longer, and the other three grown in proportion. It was a happy meeting, with their
eyes fixed upon me, and saying, as it were—
And so we have got you back again at last.

Six months' rest, with only occasional duty,
sufficed to set me up again, and place me in
the category of a discharged convalescent. I
had returned nominally in good health—that
is, I was certainly far from being on the sick
list—but a general deterioration had thinned
me down, and one had to get accustomed to
the cold and ungenial climate.

I had no time to lose now, with my children
to educate; and so, having arrived in March,
I found myself again in harness in October.

My requirements were a church in good
order and a respectable dwelling. I met with
more than both, for I found myself with two
churches.

The latter was in very far from a satis-
factory state, so here was something to set to
work at. The rector for whom I was acting

at the end of two years resigned the vicarage, and the Lord Chancellor bid me

> " Go, take possession of the church porch door,
>   And ring thy bells,"

as sings good Bishop Hall.

The church of Hatfield, in the prettily-wooded county of Hereford, presents little of interest, with the exception of some curious old monuments ·with quaint inscriptions, of the Burnam family. This ancient and honourable family date back to A.D. 1100, and still have a descendant in the person of Robert Burnham, Esq., of Long-Meadows, Mass., U.S. America. The Hatfield estate, comprising nearly the whole village, is now in the possession of the Ashton family, who have restored the chancel, and no less generously the impropriated tithe. The nave of the church is in a very dilapidated condition as regards the roof, and must shortly be restored, which makes one desire that the living were something better than a "nominal preferment." The churchyard is a pretty spot, and there, according to the parish register,

"*Anne Cleeton, being a poor wandering woman, was buried on the 1st of May, 1631.*"

Poor soul! at rest at last in a weary land!

In 1666 an Act of Parliament ordered all corpses to be buried in woollen shrouds, and the following was the curious formula used in the parish registers of that day.

"A. B., of the parish of ———, maketh oath that C. D., of the parish of ———, in the county of ———, lately deceased, was not put in, wrapt or wound up, or buried, in any shirt, shift, or sheet, or shroud made or mingled with flax, hemp, silk, hair, gold or silver, or other than what is made of sheep's wool only, nor in any coffin lined or faced with any cloth, stuff, or any other thing whatsoever, made or mingled with flax, hemp, silk, hair, gold or silver, or any other material contrary to the late Act of Parliament for burying in woollen. Dated the ——— day of ——— 1680."

And now my brief history is told. Let no one fear going out to India who is temperate in his habits and active in mind and body.

There is abundance of work to be done,

whether it be by military man or civilian. It is a glorious country, with a wondrous variety of climate and unceasing wonders, taking one back long prior to the time when Englishmen wore paint and worshipped at Stonehenge. It has peculiar attractions for the antiquary and man of science; and a fascination to the ambassador of Christ almost beyond belief.

I cannot conclude this volume better than in the words of the talented authoress of "Unbeaten Tracks in Japan," using her words with reference to India.

"Our Lord's command, 'Go ye into all the world' and preach the Gospel to every creature,' was never better defined than by the Duke of Wellington in the famous phrase in which he called it the 'marching orders of the church.'

"Widely as we may differ in theory regarding the ultimate destiny of the heathen, 'all who profess and call themselves Christians' agree that it is the church's duty to fulfil Christ's injunction with unquestioning obedience, leaving the issue to Him.

" It is one thing, however, to take a conventional interest in foreign missions at home, and another to consider them in presence of millions of heathens. In the latter case one is haunted by a perpetual sense of shame, first for one's own selfishness and apathy thousands of times multiplied, which are content to enjoy the temporal blessings by which Christianity has been accompanied, and ' the hope of life and immortality,' unembittered by the thought of the hundreds of millions, who are living and dying without these blessings and this hope."

And now, kind reader, " I hold it fit that we shake hands and part."

FINIS.

www.ingramcontent.com/pod-product-compliance
Lightning Source LLC
Chambersburg PA
CBHW021530110726
47902CB00004B/815